To Christine

…OF

EASTWOLD BY THE SEA MYSTERIES

BOOK ONE

CASSIE RUSH

all the

best

Cassie Rush

Published: February 2022

Gordian Knot Publishing

Paperback ISBN 978-1-9161221-8-5

Created with Vellum

CONTENTS

CHAPTER ONE

District Nurse Alina Merrycott looked at the patient notes clutched in her hand and grimaced. Old Cedric Mahoney's gout was still causing him incredible pain, and her lunchtime visit to change his dressings would do little to improve his discomfort. Scribbled in red pen, there was a warning remark: "Keep his walking stick out of reach. He hits people." *Come on, Alina, chin up. You've dealt with worse than him in your time.*

Drawing her shoulders back, she raised her fist to knock on the door just as Linda Cranford, the harried Meals on Wheels volunteer, opened it to leave.

'Good morning, Linda. How are you?' Alina asked, nimbly jumping aside, allowing Linda to push her basket ahead of her so she could squeeze out of the narrow doorway. Alina's stomach rumbled. A reminder that she'd missed lunch.

'Busy as ever, and it's already afternoon,' Linda replied, briskly. She removed her white caterers' trilby to waft it at a large buzzing insect, then hurried down the path, jamming her hat firmly onto her head so it didn't blow away. A wisp of mousy brown hair escaped, floating around her face as it was caught in a sea breeze. Linda stopped at the gate, removing her hand from the hat to open the latch. She turned, her light blue eyes squinting in the sunshine. 'Careful,' she said. 'He's in a bit of a grump today.'

Alina opened her mouth to reply, but Linda had already rushed away to her next client. She smiled. *When was Cedric Mahoney anything else?* She called out a cheery greeting to the old man as she stepped into the tight hallway of the tiny Victorian cottage. She heaved her medical bag into the sitting room, placed it on the sofa, and watched as the dust motes rose in a cloud. Cedric refused to have help to clean the cottage, but since it was now impossible for him to walk—thanks to his gout and the recent surgery—he definitely needed help. She made a mental note to call Kriya Andhra, the social worker, later.

'How are you, Cedric?' she said. 'Did you have a nice lunch?'

The old man simply glowered at her. His rheumy, pale green eyes narrowed under bushy white eyebrows. 'She brought me fish. I hate fish,' he grumbled.

'You ate most of it, though,' said Alina, noticing the clean plate. 'That's good.'

'I was hungry, wasn't I?' he replied. 'Can't bear to see waste.'

Alina nodded in reply but kept her thoughts to herself. She took a few disposable gloves from her bag and popped two of them on the dark brown carpet. Then she slipped her hands into another pair before kneeling on the ones on the floor to attend to his dressings. Both she and Cedric winced as she unwrapped the bandages, uncovering the surgery site from where the tophi lumps, caused by the gout, had been removed. Holding her breath she took the final dressing from his big toe. The red line from the surgeon's blade was stark against the old man's pale skin, but there was no sign of swelling or infection.

'That one's healing up nicely, Cedric,' said Alina. 'How are you getting on with the medication?'

The old man narrowed his eyes and Alina made a very unchristian remark under her breath when his walking stick collided with her shoulder. She bowed her head, biting back the tears of pain, knowing she should have paid attention to the warning on his records, and put the heavy wooden cane out of reach. It would be dreadful publicity if a nurse, let alone one who was also a part-time vicar, were to be arrested for assaulting an elderly patient, regardless of how much she'd been goaded.

The uric acid crystals forming around the old man's toe joints would make his feet feel as if they were constantly on fire. It really wasn't her intention to cause him unnecessary pain when she changed the dressings. She would need to put some arnica oil on her shoulder, especially if she was to wear the little black off-the-shoulder number she'd picked up from Melody Bell's Eastwold Emporium to the golf club dinner-dance tomorrow night. It was a little slinkier than she normally wore, but Melody was an excellent saleswoman and Alina had to admit she felt good in the dress. At a mere five feet two inches, plus a few additional and unwanted pounds, she was never going to be willowy, but the black dress made her feel wonderful—almost sexy. Well, sensual at least.

She shook her head, bringing herself back to the here and now and Mr Mahoney's feet. He braced himself, readying for the next raft of pain. She did not disappoint. In amongst his yells she heard a beeping sound. Persistent. Irritating and getting louder.

'Aren't you going to answer that thing?' Mr Mahoney shouted.

'Pardon?' said Alina, suddenly realising that the noise was her phone. She pulled it out of her medical bag and stared at the reminder.

Daisy and Aaron's wedding—3pm.

She muffled a squeal of anguish but noticed that it was not quite one-thirty. She had plenty of time to get to her other job. As long as redressing Mr Mahoney's other foot went well, she might even manage some lunch. She placed the walking stick out of reach and removed the dressings. She bathed the wound site and redressed his foot. 'You do need to keep taking the tablets, Cedric,' she said. 'How's your diet?'

'I want some steak,' muttered the old man. 'I can't stand all this rabbit food the Meals on Wheels woman brings me. If that's what she fed her husband, it's no wonder he left.'

'You know red meat isn't good for you, though. It builds up the uric acid and the gout will flare up again.' Alina reached out behind her kneeling position and used Mr Mahoney's stick to push herself up from the floor. She bent down, peeled the two gloves from the carpet, shuddered at the brown stickiness left on them and put them in the bin bag. At least the mess hadn't soaked through her trousers and onto her skin.

'I'll see you after the weekend, Cedric,' Alina said, ensuring his walking stick was back within reach. Not that he'd be walking anywhere. She made a mental note to warn the care team who'd be putting him to bed that he might be more irritable than usual this evening.

'You not going to make me a cuppa?' Cedric grumbled. 'Dr Miriam always makes me a cup of tea *and* she stops for a chat. She keeps me up to date with everything that's going on.' He stuck out his bottom lip and reached for his cane.

Alina glanced at her watch. She could make time. Despite

the number of people she saw throughout the day, she knew what loneliness felt like.

Patting her pocket to ensure she had more gloves in there, she strolled into the kitchen, bracing herself for what she expected to face. Putting the gloves on, she filled the kettle, rinsed out the teapot and scrubbed at a couple of teacups. She was surprised to find fresh milk in the fridge, briefly wondering if it was from Meals on Wheels or the night team. She'd stay for a quick chat and be on her way. There would be no time for lunch.

After washing up the teacups, Alina stepped outside Cedric's cottage and pulled the door shut. Shards of flaking paint dropped to the doorstep and were caught in a small eddy. They whirled around in a miniature maelstrom. The paintwork here was a stark contrast to the other neat cottages in the row.

Shielding her eyes, she looked out towards the sea. White-crested waves galloped towards the beach, and she heard the crash as they hit the groynes that protected the sandy cliff base from erosion. The fence, supposed to protect people and their dogs from falling over the edge of the cliff was loose in places; posts hung precariously in mid-air.

Alina took a deep breath of fresh sea air, which tugged at the neat bun on the nape of her neck. Rubbing her shoulders, she eased out some kinks and stretched. After several years working in a busy London hospital, she was still getting used to the salty crispness of Eastwold. In many ways it reminded her of her hometown of Bournemouth, but here, on the Suffolk coast, the North Sea was much colder than the English Channel, bringing with it bitterly brisk breezes despite the summer sun. Out of the corner of her eye, Alina spotted a hovering seagull poised to dive-bomb her. She ducked as she scampered along the road to her car, flinging her bag on the back seat and taking refuge in the front. The hungry gull realised it had lost out this time and, with the despairing cry of a howling child, it wheeled away, rising high on a thermal as it searched for a tasty morsel to steal from its next victim.

Shivering, Alina peered through the windscreen after it. One memory floated into her mind. The screech from a particularly large gull and her suddenly empty ice cream cone…

The phone bleeped again and she snatched it up, noticing with an anguished squeal that there was only half an hour until the wedding and she would have no time to eat anything at all. 'Please, please, please,' Alina whispered, as she placed her key in the ignition.

Delia, her burgundy and grey Citroën Dolly, was temperamental. Sometimes her engine would turn over without problems but increasingly there seemed a need for divine intervention. She turned the key. The engine coughed. Pumping the accelerator, she turned the key again. *You'll flood it.* She heard Jake as clearly as if he were sitting next to her. She glared at the empty passenger seat, stroked the steering wheel, and prayed. Delia shuddered into life and they were soon chugging away from the sea towards the parish church of St Edmund the Martyr.

She was going to make it to the wedding after all. *Well,* she grinned, her green eyes sparkling as she tucked an unruly red curl behind her ear, *it's not as if they can really start without me.*

CHAPTER TWO

Delia shuddered to a halt in a street near to St Edmund's Church. Alina thanked the car, patting the dashboard affectionately before hurrying into the church through the side door. It was ten minutes to three. Joanne Stokes, her verger, helped her struggle out of her district nurse's uniform and into the white surplice and wedding vestments.

'Cup of tea, Vicar?' said Joanne. 'Biscuit?'

'No time,' said Alina. Her stomach rumbled. Joanne furrowed her brow and placed a restraining hand on Alina's forearm.

'I think you should make time, Alina,' she said, crinkles forming around her light brown eyes. 'We can't be having noises like that in the middle of the vows, can we?'

'I suppose you're right,' Alina shrugged. 'It'll have to be a quick one, though.'

Joanne flipped the switch on the vestry kettle and opened the biscuit tin. Alina reached in, grabbed three Rich Teas, and scoffed them hurriedly, brushing crumbs away. *There goes the diet again.* She leaned forward, holding the teacup well away from her white vestments and drank, grateful that the milk had cooled the hot liquid so she didn't scald her tongue.

After her snatched snack, Alina strolled from the vestry towards the alter. Joanne had been right; not only had the biscuits filled a hole, but taking time to drink the tea had also calmed her. Nothing, however, calmed her like walking into the main body of the church. She raised her head, staring at the blue, richly painted ceiling, biting back her usual gasp of pleasure at the golden angels forming the beams. A shaft of sunlight shone through a stained glass window, glittering on the back of the pew, polished by the passing hands of many parishioners. There were no dust motes floating here. Mrs Sullivan, who cleaned the church and her own humble cottage would not allow them to remain.

Alina passed the altar to look down the aisle, nodding at the congregation who were gathering. Her hands flew to her mouth and tears pricked her eyes.

The flower ladies, as they used to jokingly call themselves, had excelled. At the end of each pew, an ivory ribbon secured a bouquet of purple freesias, mauve lisianthus and ivory roses. At the rear of the church, tall vases standing on the bookcases behind the pews were filled with yellow roses and creamy lilies. A sprig of orchids had been pushed into one vase. Alina gasped, her hand flying to her mouth. Blinking, she stared at the flowers. There were no orchids. It was just her imagination.

Relieved but with heart still pounding, Alina wandered to the flowers, breathing in the intoxicating scent. She hoped they would last until the Sunday services.

The groom, Aaron, uncomfortable in a morning suit, paced near the front pews. He ran his finger between the collar and his neck. *How long has he been here?* thought Alina, noticing the grubby grey of the collar. *Oh well, not long to go.*

She was on the verge of going over to him to chat, but at a signal from the narthex, Wilf Seward played the first few notes of the bridal march and the entire congregation stood, heads turned, waiting for Daisy's arrival.

When she appeared, everyone gasped. All brides should look beautiful on their special day, but Daisy looked exceptional. The ladies from the Eastwold Women's Guild had done her proud. Unable to afford a dress for her special day, they had offered to create one for her. Alina knew it was an amalgamation of many different wedding dresses from many bridal eras, but the end result was stunning. Most of the material had been cut on the bias, so it clung in all the right places and skimmed the floor as she passed. Daisy walked herself down the aisle with her twins ahead of her; Kylie sprinkling petals and Jason carrying the rings on a cushion. Alina batted away her own tears. She touched her wedding ring under her service book, recalling another time. Another wedding. Her beautiful bouquet of orchids. Looking down, she could scarcely see the words in her prayer book, let alone the rings on the cushion Jason was holding so proudly. She blinked and brushed the warm tears away with the corner of her stole. She knew she wasn't the only person in the congregation to feel emotional. Many residents had been at Daisy's first wedding to her childhood sweetheart, and the funeral after his death due to the weight of a tractor collapsing into a drainage ditch. By the time Alina announced, 'You may now kiss the bride,' there wasn't a dry eye in the house.

Alina led the procession into the sunshine as the young couple left the church. She waited at the door to greet the congregation, posed for photographs and, as she waved the last person goodbye, she felt a presence at her elbow.

'Not a bad job for your first wedding, Vicar,' said Wilf Seward. 'But trust a woman vicar to cry at a wedding.'

'It's only hay fever,' Alina replied, her fingers crossed in the folds of her vestments. Wilf however, hands thrust deep into his pockets, was already mounting the steps of the St Edmund's Arms. Stony faced, she folded her arms and stared after him.

'Don't mind Wilf,' said Major Fitzgerald. 'He's got a lot on his mind. I thought it was a lovely service.'

'Thank you, Major Fitzgerald,' replied Alina. 'I see you weren't needed after all.' The major had volunteered to give Daisy away, since she had no family close at hand to do the honours.

'No,' replied the major. 'And do call me Fitz. Everyone does, you know.' He pulled his shirt cuffs down so they peeked out under his tweed jacket. 'And now I think I'll join Wilf for a snifter. Can I tempt you?' He smoothed his short grey hair before putting on a tweed flat cap.

'Sorry, I have things to do at home,' replied Alina.

'Very well, I'll see you tomorrow. Seven pm sharp. I don't like stragglers.'

'Tomorrow?' Alina gave him a quick glance. *What have I forgotten now? An afternoon Parish council meeting ahead of the dance, perhaps?* The major was involved in all aspects of village life—church warden and Chair of the parish council; she could have forgotten anything. He was, however, the first friend she had made since she'd moved here, and she valued his company and his support at the parish council meetings.

'The golf club dinner-dance,' he said. 'I'm your lift. Seven o'clock.' He touched his fingertips to the peak of his cap and sauntered towards the pub.

. . .

Alina ambled back into the church, expecting to enjoy the cool peace of the empty building. She still had her sermon to write for Sunday and was struggling with the theme. As she was about to stroll to the altar and have a chat with her boss —she liked to think of Him as her boss—she heard loud voices coming from the kitchen area near the vestry.

'What *were* you thinking? I ordered African violets and you used freesias instead.'

'There were no violets, Kitty,' came the reply. 'I used what was available.'

'But freesias are so common, and they don't go with the roses at all.'

Alina sighed at the all too familiar whine of Kitty Blenkinsop. A recent addition to the coastal town of Eastwold by the Sea, Mrs Blenkinsop had thrown herself into the small town's community affairs. There were other affairs too, if you listened to the gossip, but Alina preferred to refrain from tittle-tattle.

Bracing herself for battle, Alina peered around the door to the kitchen.

'Hello ladies,' she said. 'The flowers looked wonderful. Thank you so much for all your hard work.'

'Hello, Vicar,' the three women replied. At least Amy Pretty, the wool shop owner, and Fiona Pomeroy from the flower shop looked ashamed of squabbling in church. Mrs Blenkinsop, as usual, was puffed up like a cockerel, her large bosom heaving.

'I have to say, Amy, I was particularly impressed with Daisy's dress. She looked stunning.' Alina was determined to stop the argument, whatever it had been about. But she hated confrontations and usually found a roundabout way to circumvent any such thing.

Amy Pretty blushed, patting her white hair. 'Oh thank you, Vicar,' she said. 'It was really kind of you to donate the lace. So pretty, I thought. Oh, and that yarn you ordered has come in. I've put it to one side for you.'

Kitty Blenkinsop snorted with derision. 'The dress looked just what it was. A mess of material made from a bunch of discarded gowns,' she said, batting a wasp away from her face. 'And you'd make better use of your money if you shopped online, Vicar.'

'Not quite true, Kitty,' said Alina, noticing the colour rise in Amy's cheeks. 'Firstly, I thought Daisy looked very fetching; secondly, I like to support local businesses. And the flowers were lovely, Fiona. Will they last until Sunday?'

Kitty folded her arms. 'They barely lasted through today.'

Fiona scowled at Kitty Blenkinsop. Everyone knew that her shop, Flowers by Fifi, always donated the blooms. She opened her mouth as if to reply, but simply nodded to Amy and Alina, and stalked out. The sound of her sturdy shoes clopping on the stone floor faded away.

Kitty squished the now dead wasp under the toe of her Manolo Blahniks. 'What's her problem?'

'I hardly think it's secret!' said Amy, placing her hands on her hips.

Alina glanced at both women. Kitty's calm demeanour contrasted sharply with Amy's reddened face. *What is going on?*

'We all have secrets,' said Kitty, sidling towards her. 'Don't we, Vicar?'

Alina gasped as heat stole up her face. *Don't be daft, she can't know anything.* Clenching her fists in the folds of her surplice, her stomach rumbled, reminding her she'd had no lunch; she still had an unwritten sermon and her evening meal to organise. Out of habit, she felt on her chest for her watch. Blast, she thought, it's in the vestry.

'I must go.' Alina nodded to the remaining two women, escaped into the vestry, and changed out of her vestments in double-quick time. She hung them in the wardrobe and dressed again in her nurse's uniform. 'Good job I'm still a quick-change artist,' she muttered to Joanne. 'It takes me back to my days in the amateur dramatics society, at university. Do you want a lift, Jo? I'm taking Amy back too.'

Joanne smiled her thanks and, snatching her keys from the battered desk, Alina trotted outside to Delia in order to make her way into the centre of the small town to collect something for dinner.

CHAPTER THREE

'Did I hear raised voices in the church before you came back to change?' asked Joanne. 'I thought I heard something of a kerfuffle.'

'Hmm?' said Alina, slowing the car and pulling into a passing place to allow the oncoming tractor enough room. 'Oh, it was just Kitty letting off steam again.' She glanced at Amy Pretty's impassive face in her rear-view mirror.

'What wasn't good enough for her this time?'

'The dress and the flowers, but perhaps not in that order,' replied Alina.

'I'm surprised someone hasn't swung for that woman. She's upset the whole town from what I hear,' said Jo. She sat upright in the passenger seat, her knees pressed together, her slim legs scarcely long enough for her feet to reach the floor.

'Hopefully not in the church,' replied Alina. 'That would be too much.'

Joanne giggled. 'You mustn't think badly of us, Vicar,' she said. 'We simply don't seem to be able to meet Kitty's high standards.'

On the back seat, Amy snorted. 'If she'd done to me what she's doing to Fiona, I'd cheerfully kill her.'

Glancing in her rear-view mirror, Alina was tempted to ask more about the friction between Kitty and Fiona. The old lady, however, stared out the car window as if nothing had happened. Alina began peering through the windscreen to focus on the narrow roads leading to the town centre. Finding a solitary free parking space in the town square, she swung Delia into it, patted the steering wheel and turned off the engine. Battling with Amy's enormous handbag, Alina helped her clamber off the rear seat and watched her toddle safely across the road to her wool shop.

Locking the car, Alina noticed the air was fragrant with the aroma of frying batter. Salt from the sea air mingled with the scent of malt vinegar, and Alina's mouth watered. Frank Stokes, Joanne's husband, had already started frying. With her stomach growling, Alina followed Joanne to their fish and chip shop. Cod and chips, she thought. Not a finer supper on the earth.

'Hello, Frank,' said Alina as she stepped into the shop, and breathed in the intoxicating scent of frying batter, crisping potatoes, salt and vinegar.

He looked up from his task of sliding battered pieces of cod into the sizzling oil. 'Hi there, Vicar. How was the wedding?' He narrowed his eyes, following his wife's passage to the rear quarters.

'Most of it went very well, thanks Frank,' Alina replied.

'Most?' said Frank. He arched one eyebrow.

'Yes, one person wasn't too happy about the flowers, but at least the bride and groom had left by then.'

'Ah. That would be Mrs B, wouldn't it?' Frank smirked. 'She's going to upset the wrong person one day.' He cleared his throat and looked at the forming queue. 'Cod and chips for one?'

'Yes please, Frank,' she replied, nodding at some of the locals who'd had the same idea for supper. There were a few couples she didn't recognise. Grockles, she decided. Tourists, in other words. The locals weren't unfriendly, but there were frustrations over large cars and even larger caravans taking over the small lanes around Eastwold. Farmers were always so busy; they didn't like being held up. Same with the fisher folk. Important to get fish to market at its freshest. Although both industries usually took place long before most tourists rose in the morning, there were still regular altercations.

Envy, she thought. *Was that a good theme?* Thinking back to the argument in the church, she toyed with the idea of Wrath. What had they been arguing about? Surely not just the flowers. She sighed, once again wondering if she'd made the right decision to leave London. She was happy enough here in Eastwold. Claire, her daughter, had been placed in Meredith College, a good local boarding school paid for by Alina's ever-generous parents. This meant Alina could focus on her patients and parishioners during term-time. Scratching her head, she thought back to the scene in the church. There was something underlying the tension that was about more than flowers. *What on earth is going on between Kitty and Fiona? And why is Amy involved?*

'Vicar?' Frank stood, a parcel wrapped in plain paper on the stainless steel counter in front of him. Her supper. She paid with a debit card, took her parcel, and placed it under her arm. Her car would be safe enough where it was parked. It was often difficult to get a parking place near her little cottage. She ambled around the corner and into the cul-de-sac where Lighthouse Cottage, painted in a shade known as Suffolk Blue, squatted beneath its whitewashed neighbour. The lighthouse was an imposing building, dwarfing her little cottage. She hoped that its foundations were stronger than the one down the coast, which had been dismantled before it was swept away into the sea. They were not far above the tide line here in Mill Lane, but she'd been told the tide rarely rose high enough to reach her front garden. *Time will tell, I suppose.*

She opened the front door and, as she kicked off her shoes, she was immediately assailed by meowing and protests from Thalia, her Siamese cat.

'Yes, I'm sure there'll be enough for you,' she said, bending down to stroke the silky cream and brown fur. Perhaps Greed, she thought. But no, that wasn't fair. The cat was just hungry and, apart from Mrs Sullivan popping in to clean, Thalia had been alone all day.

Thalia sniffed at the parcel and, glaring at Alina, padded through the sitting room into the kitchen-dining area. She sat by her bowl, an accusing expression on her face.

'You always make me feel so guilty,' muttered Alina.

'Meow,' said Thalia, looking from her bowl to her hand slave, and back again.

Alina collected a plate and cutlery from the Welsh dresser, which had been her grandmother's. She ran her fingertips over the scratched wood. Claire had painted it with a Farrow and Ball chalk paint during her last holiday. Alina wasn't sure if it was an improvement or not. She'd loved the battered pine, but she had to agree the fresh yellow tones brightened up the kitchen.

'Meow,' said Thalia, a little more insistently. Alina opened the parcel, removed her fish, scooped half the chips onto her plate and placed the knife and fork alongside the fish. With her fingers she removed the batter and pulled a section of the white fish away. She mashed it in Thalia's bowl.

'Careful,' she said to the cat, placing the bowl on the floor again. 'It's hot.'

The cat merely glanced at her. Alina imagined the words "I know" from the cat's expression.

'Oh, why do I always leave it to the last minute?' she sighed.

Thalia, her pink tongue snatching morsels of fish, didn't reply.

Alina put her plate on a tray, fetched herself a glass of water and wandered into a small sitting room. 'What can I talk about this week?' she said. She ate her supper sitting on a small sofa, sipping the water. When she'd eaten, she took the tray into the kitchen and rinsed everything before placing it in the dishwasher. Back in her sitting room she picked up a notebook, turning to the last page she'd written upon: 'Seven Deadly Sins' was the title scrawled at the top. There was nothing else. She wrote down Wrath, Envy and Greed. Her pencil was poised, but her mind was a complete blank.

Alina stretched her legs out, then tucked them up underneath her and curled up with Thalia. A photograph of Claire looked at her from the side table beside the sofa. As she reached out to touch it, her landline rang.

'Claire, darling,' she said, when she heard the voice. 'I was just thinking about you.'

'What are you up to?' asked Claire.

'Thinking about my sermon,' replied Alina, biting her bottom lip.

'Oh, Mum! How often do you moan about me leaving *my* homework to the last minute?'

'I know, I know. I thought the seven deadly sins would be easy, but I can't find a single sin to focus on.'

'The deadly sins? That's a bit heavy, isn't it?' Claire sniggered. 'What *were* you thinking?'

'About repentance, penitence and forgiveness, I suppose,' replied Alina. She held the handset away from her ear as Claire burst into laughter.

'You've broken your diet again, haven't you?'

'When did you become so smart?' Alina smiled. It was good to hear Claire laugh again. She'd been angry about moving away from her old school, but it had become necessary under the circumstances.

'I'm fourteen, Mum. I know how your mind works. I still think it's a bit heavy.'

'You may be right, but I've left it a bit late now…'

'You should do your homework when it's given to you.' Claire's voice took on a knowing I-told-you-so tone.

'Yes, okay. Perhaps you're right. Are you still coming home next weekend?'

'Yes, I am. Can't wait to see you.'

'Me too. Love you to the moon and back.'

'Listen Mum, I've gotta go. Love you too. Bye.'

The line went dead, but Alina held the handset to her ear until the phone went back to the dialling tone. She replaced the handset, thinking about another phone call, many years before, when she'd reported Jake as a missing person. She'd been surprised and then angry that the police had said he was an adult, not in any immediate danger, and that they'd wait twenty-four hours before looking for him. Screeching in the background came the howls of baby Claire. The police officer had simply asked, 'That your baby?' and in response to Alina's whispered 'Yes,' he'd said, 'Hardly a surprise he's done a runner then, is it?'

Blinking away her tears, she picked up Thalia and held the cat close to her heart.

CHAPTER FOUR

Whilst the following morning dawned bright and clear, a cloud still hung over Alina. She was unsure which one of the seven deadly sins to include in her sermon. After wandering around the house, staring out of the windows at the tiny courtyard garden, she'd even picked up the new Judy Jacobs crime mystery to read a chapter—but that had led to two chapters and then three, and she'd had to force herself to put the book down. Now, she sat in her office twiddling a pencil, watching clouds out of the Velux roof lantern, and she still had no ideas. You need some fresh air, she told herself.

As it was a Saturday and she wanted to collect her knitting yarn from Pretty's Yarns and Fabrics, she decided to take a stroll around the village, or was it a town, she was never really sure. She was not on duty that morning and, unless there was a wedding, it was often the one day of the week where she tended to have very few responsibilities.

Enjoying the sunlight and breathing in the sea air, she ambled along the High Street, window shopping. A car horn beeped at her, and Joanne Stokes waved from the passenger seat—Jo and Frank, she knew, were helping with the set-up of the dining room at the golf club, and Alina didn't envy them their day in the company of Mrs Blenkinsop. Stopping to chat with various neighbours and parishioners, it reminded her of how impersonal her life in London had been. Eastwold numbered around nine hundred residents and today, it seemed as if everyone was out and about taking in the first warm days of early summer, enjoying the empty streets before the tourists arrived. It was something Alina was yet to experience, having arrived not long after the height of the tourist season was over. The population almost doubled, she'd been told. You could scarcely walk along the pavements, let alone park your car. Therefore, with one thing and another, it took her longer than she'd expected to home in on her destination.

The small bell overhead jangled as she pushed the shop door open. Alina paused for a moment, narrowing her eyes at the source of the sound. Heat rushed over her face as memories of trying to learn campanology flooded back. Bell ringing was a physical and mental exercise she'd hated. Despite always knowing which bell to ring, the young Alina frequently found herself behind, rarely picking up the correct bell. It had not made her popular with the other girls; at least, not until she left the group.

'Good morning, Vicar,' said Amy Pretty, the elderly owner of Pretty's Yarns and Fabrics. 'Have you come for your blue yarn?'

'I have, thank you Amy. So kind of you to remind me yesterday,' said Alina. 'I just wanted to say again how pretty both the church and Daisy looked yesterday.'

'Glad to hear *you* were happy, Vicar. Although it's very hard to please some.' Amy rang Alina's purchase up on the till. 'That will be £14.98, Vicar.'

Alina removed a twenty pound note from her purse and laid it in Amy's open palm.

Amy counted the change slowly into Alina's outstretched hand. 'Who are you knitting for, Vicar?' she asked.

'My sister,' replied Alina, stuffing both coin and note into her pocket. 'This is her third, or is it her fourth? You know, I can't quite remember. Fourth, I think, but I lose track.'

'Nice to have a big family,' sighed Amy. She stared over Alina's head into the distance, then shook herself, returning to the present. 'I thought the freesias looked a treat with the roses. I'm so glad you liked them, but there's always one who's not satisfied.'

Alina nodded and reached for the bag of yarn, hoping to leave quickly as she was anxious not to become embroiled in the battle between Amy Pretty and Kitty Blenkinsop. But Amy was on fire.

'You know she's taken over the quilting guild now?' the old woman whispered. Her pale blue eyes, cloudy with cataracts, were fixed on Alina.

Unable to help herself, Alina asked, 'Who?'

'Kitty Blenkinsop! The woman can't even sew but she's forced her way in there and is telling everyone else how to complete their quilts. The same with Knit and Natter. She can't knit but she's managed to get them to accept her as President. That was *my* job! Has been for years.' Amy pulled a scrap of lace handkerchief from her sleeve. She wiped her nose delicately and replaced it.

Alina regarded the sleeve bulge suspiciously. That's how germs spread, she said to herself. Aloud, she said, 'I'm sorry to hear that, Amy.'

'But that's not all.' Amy's voice rose. 'She's telling everyone to go to Ipswich or Woodbridge to shop. You heard her yesterday. She's saying to people that shopping online is much better than the choice I offer. She's ruining my business. If it keeps up, I'll have to shut the shop—then what will I do?'

'You could sell it and retire,' offered Alina.

Amy snorted. 'Who's going to want to buy a failing business. Selling the shop was my retirement fund. I have nothing else!'

This was more serious than she'd thought, Alina decided. 'Perhaps I can have a quiet word with her?' she found herself volunteering, all the while shuddering at the prospect. 'I know *I* love to buy locally and I'm sure everyone else does too. It may not be as bad as you think.'

'You can try, Vicar,' replied Amy. 'She certainly won't listen to me. My takings have been down ever since she moved here.'

'Very good,' said Alina, finally snatching up the bag of yarn. 'I'll try and talk to her. I'll see you this evening at the dinner-dance?'

Amy snapped her mouth shut. Her lips pressed into a thin line and her eyes glittered with tears.

Oh good grief, thought Alina. Of course, Kitty's taken that over as well. Placing the bag of yarn on the counter, she said, 'Shall I make you a nice cup of tea, Amy?' Perhaps it would assuage her guilt at making the old lady cry. She pushed past the beaded curtain that hung over the doorway to the small kitchen at the back of the shop. Rattling around in the kitchenette, she tried to make enough noise to cover the sound of Amy's sobs.

The shop bell chimed, indicating another customer. The voices were muted, and Alina tiptoed closer to the curtain, wondering what they were whispering about. She should have known.

Kitty Blenkinsop was the subject on everyone's lips, it appeared.

'I could kill her! I don't mind her taking Nick off my

hands—I'd grown tired of his demands. But why does she have to put me down with her snide remarks all the time? That's what I can't stand!'

'Oh, I know, dear,' Amy's voice soothed, all sounds of her own tears gone. 'But she'll get what's coming to her, you mark my words.'

Alina finished making the tea and rattled the bead curtain. The two women sprang apart. She placed the cup of tea on the counter next to Amy's left hand, nodded to Linda Cranford, and marched to the door. This she wrenched open, sucking in the sea air greedily. Envy once again came to her mind. That would make a good theme for the sermon.

CHAPTER FIVE

'Oh well, no time like the present,' Alina said to herself, already regretting her impetuosity in offering to help. *Bloody interfering*, Jake, her late husband, would have called it. Patting her pocket, she felt for her car keys. She'd drive up to the golf club and talk to Kitty. See if she could pour oil on the troubled waters. Since she's always hated confrontations, she whispered for strength from Him as she drove to the club.

Despite not being the oldest building in Eastwold—that honour lay with the parish church—the Victorian golf clubhouse doors were tall and heavy. Alina used all her weight to push against the brass handle and finally the oak and glass entrance door edged open, allowing her ingress. As she walked into the reception area, she heard raised voices. She closed her eyes and, with her heart pounding, edged towards the sound.

Kitty Blenkinsop, a clipboard clutched to her large bosom, quivered as she shouted at several men. 'I want a long top table and every other table to be round. Cabaret style! Do you understand what cabaret style means?'

'That's not what it says here, Mrs B,' said Wilf Seward. '*All* cabaret style, them be on this plan. No top table.' He thrust a sheet of paper under Mrs Blenkinsop's nose. She waved it away. The same imperious gesture used to sweep away reassurances raised over the flowers yesterday.

'That is what we agreed, Kitty,' Joanne Stokes ventured gently.

'I ran numerous major events when Mr Blenkinsop was still with us. I've always had a top table and I don't see why this event should be any different.'

'But Kitty—'

Kitty rounded on Joanne, hands on hips, 'How dare you interrupt me when I'm speaking!'

Joanne backed away, biting her lip and staring at the floor.

'Here, you can't talk to my wife like that!' Frank Stokes, his face reddening, stepped closer to Kitty.

Kitty glanced in his direction, briefly.

Alina wanted to step away and wait until the tempers had subsided. Although she hated seeing the kindly and gentle Joanne being treated with such disdain, at least Frank was standing up for her. It was the one thing she'd hated about her marriage to Jake—the shouting. Her parents never shouted. They disagreed, naturally, but never at volume.

'Kitty...?' Alina squared her shoulders and braced herself. She projected her voice as she'd learned to do in the university am-dram club. 'Mrs Blenkinsop, perhaps we could have a quiet word?'

For a large woman, Kitty Blenkinsop had a surprising turn of speed. She whirled around, and in two strides was face to face with Alina. She squinted down at the shorter woman, her bosom still heaving.

Alina bunched her fingers tightly, transported back to her school years. It was Susan Grainger all over again, but she wasn't ten any longer and she'd learnt to stand up to bullies. 'P-perhaps we could have a quiet word,' Alina repeated.

'About?' said Kitty, haughtily.

Alina shuddered and reached up to wipe Kitty's spittle from her cheek with a tissue. She stood her ground. 'It's about the Eastwold Women's Guild—'

'It'll have to wait,' replied Kitty, turning away.

'I think now would be a good time,' Alina replied. 'Perhaps give these men a chance to finish setting up the ballroom.'

'They're doing it wrong,' sneered Kitty.

'I'm sure they'll be fine,' replied Alina. 'Shall we?'

'No,' replied Kitty. 'We shall not. I've got work to do, Vicar, even if you haven't.' She turned in the direction of the ballroom and stomped away. Seconds later she was heard yelling at the men who had taken the opportunity to carry on setting up the tables.

'Cup of tea, Vicar?' A soft voice sounded at her elbow, and Alina readily agreed and followed Wilf Seward's wife, Dot, to the kitchen and away from the arguments.

'You've done it now,' said Dot, pouring hot water from the urn into a teapot. 'She's a real witch, that one. She'll be gunning for you next.'

'For me?' said Alina in alarm. 'Why me?'

'She doesn't like anyone disagreeing with her. You were against her over the flowers yesterday, or so I hear?' Dot swilled water around the teapot and then tipped it down the sink. Satisfied that the teapot was warm enough, she placed three large spoons of tealeaves into the pot, poured in more boiling water from the urn and rested a folded tea towel over the top. Cups and saucers she took from the cupboard, placing them on the table, and poured fresh milk into a white jug.

'You certainly know your way around this kitchen, Dot,' said Alina, running her fingertips over the stainless steel tabletop.

'I worked here in my younger days,' Dot replied. 'Nothing's changed. Not like some things.' She nodded in the direction of the continued shouting, which they could still hear though the closed door.

Alina bowed her head and didn't reply. It seemed no one had taken to Kitty. But pride might be a worthy topic for her sermon... 'The ladies certainly had the church looking splendid yesterday,' she said.

'Thank you, Vicar, but even that wasn't right for her, now was it?' said Dot, pouring the tea. 'Have a biscuit. Freshly made this morning.'

'They do look very tempting,' said Alina. Blow the diet, she thought. One's not going to stop me getting in the dress tonight. She took two biscuits from the tin. They're very small, she told herself. You can resist everything except temptation, said the voice in her head. 'Shush,' she muttered.

'What was that, Vicar?' said Dot.

Alina noticed that Dot had taken one biscuit for herself and suddenly she felt very greedy, but it would be bad manners, not to mention unhygienic, if she put the biscuit back in the tin. 'Nothing,' she mumbled through biscuit crumbs. She chewed contentedly whilst listening to Dot complain about Kitty Blenkinsop.

The kitchen door burst open and Alina jumped, but it was Joanne Stokes and Linda Cranford, escaping from whatever duties Kitty must have assigned them.

'Cup of tea, ladies?' Dot asked, already pouring the hot liquid into the waiting cups.

'Dot, you're a life saver,' said Linda, smiling broadly. 'One more word and I would swing for that husband-stealing witch. I'm surprised someone hasn't done it already, hey, Jo?'

'I'm surprised you're here, given what happened,' Joanne said.

Linda gave a thin-lipped smile. 'She's not running my life for me.'

Joanne Stokes gave Linda an embarrassed smile, glancing briefly in Alina's direction.

'I'm sure the vicar doesn't want to hear us squabbling about each other,' she said.

'Oh, the vicar won't mind, will you?' said Linda. 'We're only letting off steam. No harm done.'

Alina gave them all a faint smile, half-wondering how Linda had arrived so quickly. I should stop this, she told herself, wondering which husbands other than Linda's had been stolen. She allowed herself to drift, only half-listening to the women's conversation as she sipped the hot tea.

The fridge door slammed, rattling the lids of the saucepans stored on its top.

'Why is there never any sodding milk in this house?' he yelled.

'There's a five pound note in my purse,' she whispered. 'If you'll look after Claire, I'll go and get some.'

'Sod that. The brat just bawls if I hold her. Give me the money. I suppose I'll have to go and get the blasted milk myself.' He snatched her handbag from the kitchen counter and emptied it onto the floor. Wrenching open her purse, he grabbed the blue fiver.

The front door crashed shut behind him and the saucepan lids rattled in reply.

Alina calmed her baby, the sobs softening to snuffles and, as Claire fell asleep, the freshly boiled water grew cold while the silence of the house enveloped mother and child.

. . .

At a shout of laughter from the women, Alina was snatched from her reverie. She pushed her tea away and, making her excuses, she ran for her car. Fumbling with the keys, Alina started the engine and wondered about Kitty's temper as she drove away. Had the woman always been so aggressive? She had a short temper, that much was true, but there must be a reason behind it. Wasn't there? Or perhaps not? Jake hadn't needed a reason to be angry. In the weeks after Claire's birth, he was angry all the time. But they had been very young and not getting much sleep.

It had been a relief at first, when he'd not returned from the corner shop. Then a worry, as the days turned to weeks. The police had been of very little help. Jake wasn't a danger to himself. He was in no danger from anyone else, or at least so they said. Alina thought differently, but Jake wouldn't thank her for sharing some of his activities with the police. Her husband had simply disappeared into the night, never to be seen again.

Alina shook her head, bringing herself back into the present. Jake was her past. Her unwritten sermon was her clear and present urgency.

CHAPTER SIX

'Oh Thalia,' Alina said, when the cat greeted her at the front door. 'Everyone is up in arms about Kitty Blenkinsop.'

Thalia glared but mewed her reply. Alina collected her sermon notes, followed the cat into the kitchen, and put the kettle on. She made herself a cup of tea, ensured Thalia had fresh food and water, and sat down at the dining room table. Thalia sat on a chair nearby, ignoring Alina's frown, and placed her paws on the table.

'You do know I don't like you on the kitchen table, don't you?' she said to the cat. Thalia blinked and put her head on one side. In a teenager it would have been "whatever".

'Hmm,' Alina said, reaching out to scratch the cat's head. 'Help me choose a deadly sin for my sermon?'

'Meow,' said Thalia, scratching her ear.

'Pride, you think?' she said, reaching for her bible. 'James four six, or would four ten be better? What do you think?'

Thalia sniffed at her paw and resumed scratching.

'Yes, four ten, I think you're right,' said Alina. 'Humble yourselves before the Lord, and he will exalt you.'

Thalia twisted her head around and started licking her spine. The matter, it appeared, was settled.

'Very well, since you're such a clever cat, you deserve a treat.' Alina ambled to the fridge and poured a bowl of lactose-free cream for the cat. Thalia eased herself from the chair, oozing to the floor as only a cat can, to stroll over to her bowl. Alina stroked the seal point brown head as the cat settled herself to tuck in.

Alina resumed her seat at the kitchen table, her bible in front of her and a notepad to one side. She jotted words down, crossed them out and scribbled more ideas. Sitting gazing into space, Alina chewed the end of her pencil. Perhaps she was just hungry? The kitchen clock said four o'clock. She wouldn't be eating until at least eight—a little snack couldn't do any harm, could it? Ham, tomatoes, cheese. When she'd completed building her sandwich it was quite tall. I'm going to break my jaw, she thought. She used all her weight to squish the sandwich down so she could cut it in half. Alina wandered into the sitting room and plonked herself on the sofa. Munching on the mountainous sandwich, she resumed her scribbling. Nothing more than bullet points, but she was sure inspiration would strike her once she was in the pulpit and her congregation sat expectantly before her. Resting her eyes for a moment, she prayed for the muse to pay her a visit. A flash of brilliance was all she needed. She yawned and reached out for more of her sandwich, but there were just crumbs on the plate. Her mug of tea was cold. What was the time? Half past six! How did that happen? Stretching and yawning again, her crime novel slipped from her lap. Alina groaned, realising she'd fallen asleep. The major would be here in half an hour and she was nowhere near ready.

She raced upstairs to her bedroom and put the curlers on to heat. Rushing downstairs again to the bathroom, she showered quickly, wrapped herself in a large towel, and put the hot curlers in her hair. They were not going to have long enough to make much difference in easing out her tight curls, but anything was better than nothing. Dried and half-dressed in new knickers and bra, she tried pulling on tights. After snagging the third pair she decided bare legs would have to do and she slipped the dress over her head. *Was it this short when I tried it on in the shop?* Perhaps some thick tights would be better? Or better still, a different dress entirely. This one had looked lovely in Melody Bell's shop, but now? Was it appropriate? She reached for the handle on the wardrobe when the doorbell rang. *Blast. He's early. Makeup!* Alina dashed to the window.

'Just a second, Major,' she called, acutely aware of the dress sliding up the back of her legs as she leaned forward. 'Two minutes.'

She chose to ignore the comment he made as he wandered back to his car, and pulled mascara and lipstick from a seagrass box on her dressing table. She never wore makeup as a rule. It had never been allowed when she was a young nurse, and was certainly not expected in her other job as a vicar.

She pulled the curlers from her hair, combed out the curls, and the auburn tresses caressed her shoulders. Twisting each wave around her fingers as she brushed her hair through, Alina looked at herself in the mirror. Not too bad. She grabbed the small black bag Melody Bell had insisted she buy too, stuffing lipstick and money inside. The strappy sandals were the last item and she put them on, twirled in front of the mirror and took them off again before running downstairs. After making sure that Thalia had enough food in her bowl, she dived out the front door. She put the heels on once more, took a deep breath, and strolled down the tiny pathway.

Major Fitzgerald stepped out of his car, leaned on the low, sleek roof for a moment and whistled.

'You look amazing, Vicar,' he said, as he strolled around the front of his car. The red paint sparkled in the summer sunshine. 'Or may I call you Alina, since you look very un-vicar-like this evening?'

'Yes,' Alina squeaked, backing away from him. *What's happened to my voice?* She coughed, clearing her throat, and tried again. 'Yes, by all means, call me Alina.'

'And you must call me Fitz,' he said, prowling towards her. 'Everyone does, you know.' He reached down and opened the door of the low car.

Alina squinted at the seat. *How on earth am I going to get down there?* There was, Alina knew, an art of getting into a sports car but it wasn't one that she'd had much opportunity to practise. If only the dress were a little longer. The major leaned in close and offered his hand. The smell of whisky was overpowering. Stepping back, Alina stumbled into the car seat. She hurriedly pulled her dress down to cover her thighs. The major smiled. Alina suddenly knew how a chicken felt when the fox entered the hen house. Perhaps she could get a taxi home from the golf club later?

Reaching inside the small bag, relief flowed through her as her fingers touched the smooth cover of her mobile phone. She ensured her dress wasn't showing too much of her thighs or, heaven forbid, the vicar's knickers, and put the seat belt on.

At a touch of the starter button, the engine burst into life, an initial growl settling into the purr of a large cat. 'My retirement present to myself,' murmured Major Fitzgerald.

'Very nice,' Alina said. She glanced at the steering wheel; the GT-R logo gave her no indication of the car's make. She braced herself for the jolt of the car leaping into action. It was surprisingly smooth. The engine hummed, eating up the short distance to the golf club.

Fitz dropped her at the door. 'I'll just get the old girl parked up and I'll be with you,' he said. 'Hold on there, I'll help you out.'

Alina nodded. Keeping her knees pressed together, she swung her legs out of the car as soon as the door opened. The major leaned forward and she grasped his hand, ignoring the grimace on his face as she pulled herself into a standing position.

'Thank you,' she panted. With two busy jobs, finding time for a fitness regime was impossible. She smoothed down her dress, tugging at the hem, and touched her hair. She'd slip into the ladies' and make sure she wasn't too frightful after her tussles getting in and out of the car.

With a big sigh, she carefully crossed the gravel drive to the clubhouse, walking on tiptoes to avoid digging thin heels into gravel.

CHAPTER SEVEN

Alina pushed against the weighty clubhouse doors for the second time that day and gazed around, taking in all the work that had gone on since her visit that morning. The old-fashioned chandeliers illuminated the reception area. Each crystal teardrop glinted, refracting coloured light against the white walls. They were breath-taking. Alina stood underneath them turning around, sure she'd never seen them alight before. Suddenly aware of a presence at her shoulder, she accepted a glass of champagne from a waiter but declined the offer of the hatcheck boy to take her shawl. Outside it had been a warm balmy evening, inside it was cool but definitely heating up as yet another argument was in full swing.

'Where do you think you're going?' Kitty Blenkinsop clasped the arm of a waitress.

'I need to get some clean glasses.' The young woman peeled Kitty's fingers off her forearm. Kitty's nails had left an imprint on the waitress's skin.

'You're going for a cigarette, I know you are. There's no

time and I don't want you stinking of smoke when people are trying to eat.'

'I am going to get some clean glasses. You think what you want, you old bat. You *do* what you want. I don't care anymore.' The waitress fled and slammed through the door to the kitchen, returning a few moments later with a tray of fresh glasses. She gave Kitty a smug grin and headed back into the ballroom.

'Mrs Blenkinsop, a word if you don't mind!'

Kitty sighed loudly and turned to face Ralph Pomeroy. 'You are not sitting at the top table, Ralph.' Kitty's face was puce; her bosom heaved. Alina was convinced Kitty was placing considerable strain on her undergarments as she could see the elastic digging into the woman's fleshy midriff.

'I'm the club captain,' said Ralph Pomeroy, hands on hips as he swaggered towards her. He stared down his long nose at Kitty, sneering as she took a step backwards. His face coloured as Kitty batted at him with her clipboard. He brushed it aside as if he were flicking away an irritating insect.

'I always sit at the top table,' he slurred. The clipboard fell to the floor, ripping the single sheet of paper attached to it, and Alina found herself wondering how many gins he'd had before turning up for the dinner-dance. She looked around for Fiona, hoping that she could rein in her husband's behaviour.

Kitty, open-mouthed, clutched her pearls and stared at the damaged clipboard. 'You pick that up, now!' she hissed. Her right hand, fingers spread, was pressed to her still heaving bosom. Her left hand clenched around a petite bag. The square-cut diamond on her third finger glinted as she raised her bag.

It's been quite a day, thought Alina, stepping forward,

convinced that Kitty was on the point of backhanding the club captain with her four-carat engagement ring.

'What's going on?' Fitz, by her side, pulled her back and hissed in her ear.

'Kitty,' she whispered. 'Ralph is insisting on sitting at the top table. Kitty won't let him.'

'Seems a bit harsh. He is club captain after all.' Fitz played with his cufflinks, his pink cheeks displaying his embarrassment at the show of emotion in front of him.

'I know,' sighed Alina. She picked up the clipboard from the floor. Twenty circles were drawn on it with eight names neatly typed inside each circle. Ralph and Fiona Pomeroy were at one of the three tables at the front of the room near the lectern where all the speeches would be made.

'Ralph,' she said, tapping his forearm. He swung around, still snarling. Alina stepped backwards, but he took a deep breath and calmed himself.

'Sorry, Vicar. Didn't see you there. What is it?' He swayed slightly, his eyes unfocused. Alina recalculated his gin intake, revising it to at least double figures.

'There *is* no top table this year, Ralph,' she said. 'It was agreed at the planning stage. You're here at one of the front tables, see?' She pointed at his name on the seating plan. 'We decided that round cabaret-style tables were a bit more sociable.'

'I see, Vicar. I've no idea why Mrs Blenkinsop couldn't have explained that to me herself.' He pulled at his lapels, straightened his dinner jacket and fiddled with the bow tie.

'Ralph, leave it alone,' said Fiona Pomeroy. She stood in front of him, slapped his hands away from the bow and reached up to tweak his tie. 'There, that's better,' she said, patting him on the chest.

Alina smiled. Where had Fiona been up until now, she wondered. Perhaps much of this could have been avoided.

Ralph kissed his wife on the forehead. Whatever Fiona had done he was calmer, breathing more slowly, and the flush on his cheeks was fading.

Alina looked around for the major and saw him strolling into the dining room. Kitty Blenkinsop was hanging off his arm.

'That's what she does, I'm afraid, Vicar,' Fiona said, her arm linked through her husband's.

'I beg your pardon?' replied Alina.

'Any man she can get her claws into…'

'Well the major isn't really mine to steal,' Alina said.

'Don't tell Kitty that, or she'll throw him back.'

'Let's go in, dear,' slurred Ralph. He glowered at Kitty's retreating back.

Perhaps wrath would make a better topic after all, thought Alina, still worrying about her sermon. But it was all too late now, she berated herself, taking another sip of champagne and ambling to her seat in the centre of the room where she'd been placed next to Major Fitzgerald. He rose to pull out her chair. Smiling, she smoothed her dress underneath her bottom before she sat and pulled the hem closer to her knees.

'You look very nice, Vicar.' Dot Seward leaned around her husband to speak to Alina. Wilf snorted. With derision? Alina wondered. Wilf was one of the villagers she still had to warm to. *You must get a grip. It's only a dress.*

'Thank you,' she whispered to Dot. 'It's a bit shorter than I'm used to. But Melody talked me into it.'

'Did I hear my name?' Melody Bell, champagne in hand, swooped in to kiss Alina on both cheeks. 'You look lovely, and don't let anyone else tell you any different. Stand up and give me a twirl. Oh my goodness, look at those legs, Vicar. You should get those out more often.'

Alina dipped her head; heat rose up her neck and flamed across her face. 'Please don't,' she begged.

But Melody ignored her pleas. 'Doesn't she look lovely, Major Fitz?' Melody winked at Alina, as Fitz choked on his gin and tonic. 'Yes, yes, splendid,' he replied.

I am never going to live this down, thought Alina. She plonked herself in her chair, trying to pull the dress so it covered her knees. There wasn't enough material, so she plucked the napkin from the table and used that to cover her lap instead. Out of the corner of her eye, she saw the major pout with disappointment. She shook her head. Why didn't I wear trousers, she asked herself. *This is going to be a night I shall never forget.*

CHAPTER EIGHT

Alina closed her eyes in bliss, grinning to herself as she tucked into roast beef, crisp Yorkshire puddings and all the trimmings. A roast was one of her favourite meals, but always too much trouble for one person, The potatoes were a little disappointing, however; slightly under-done, and they had not been roughed up like the local cooking guru, Delilah Smythe, recommended. It really does make such a difference crisping the outside, thought Alina. An incredibly simple thing. But of course, the catering-sized saucepans would be far too heavy for someone to shake, even after draining the boiling water away.

'Oh, no more, thank you Major,' she said, covering the top of her wine glass before he could top it up again. 'I've lost count of how many I've had. I have a service and a sermon to deliver in the morning, you know. It wouldn't be right for the vicar to intoxicate the first three rows with just her breath.'

'Fair enough, Alina, but it is good to see you enjoying yourself. I do like a woman who enjoys her food. I hate to see a woman wasting away.'

Not much chance of that, thought Alina, catching him staring at her cleavage. *Melody Bell, I shall never forgive you for this! I thought this dress was a bit too revealing, but I let you talk me into buying it. I'll never live this down!* She laid her knife and fork next to each other on her clean plate. Perhaps I can forgo dessert, she thought. But when the sliver of Key Lime pie was placed in front of her, she convinced herself it was rude to refuse. Promising herself she'd dance it off after the speeches, Alina sat back, enjoying the fact that someone else was getting up on their hind legs to address the gathering for once.

At the lectern, Kitty Blenkinsop tapped a spoon against the side of her wine glass. The microphone screeched and everyone covered their ears and glared at her. Unabashed, Kitty put the glass down and tapped the microphone instead. It screeched again and Bert Rigg, the local police officer, raced to the front.

'It's fine, woman,' the audience heard him hiss. 'Stop tapping it, you're making things worse. Stand back, keep your hands off the mic and it will work just fine.'

Bert stalked away from the microphone and sat back at a table in the middle of the room. Alina saw him lean over and whisper something to his wife. She laughed, hiding her smile behind her hands, then shared the joke with Linda Cranford. Linda guffawed loudly, glaring at Kitty as if daring her to chastise her merriment.

Kitty began her speech, thanking everyone for their support. It was not inspiring, and Alina found herself looking around the room to see who was there and who was missing. Just the great and the good, thought Alina. *I suppose I should think myself lucky that I was included.* She giggled to herself. There had been a time when she would not have been caught dead in company like this.

I wonder what they would think if they knew about the squat? she wondered. No, none of them would understand. No one sitting down at least. Standing around the edge of the room were the waiting staff who'd brought food, refilled glasses, and carried away the empty dishes. Matching uniforms and matching bored expressions as Kitty continued to talk. I wonder if they'd understand about those days, Alina thought to herself. She gazed around the young faces, stopping at one. The young woman who had argued with Kitty before dinner was still glowering. If looks could kill, thought Alina, she would be the one who did it. She rested her arm along the back of her chair, watching the young woman and wondering what the history was between her and Kitty Blenkinsop.

Suddenly everyone was clapping and Alina was dragged out of her daydream. Was it over? But it was only a temporary reprieve. Kitty held a large plastic bucket—of course, the raffle prizes, followed by an auction. Alina would have groaned aloud, but all the money being raised was for the church roof. Her church roof and the beautiful ceiling that the roof protected. Instead, she simply closed her eyes, imagining a beatific smile on her face. By the time the raffle and auction were over, Alina had imbibed some of the bliss her smile had given out.

Encouraged onto the dance floor by her parishioners, Alina found herself clutched in a tight embrace with Major Fitzgerald. She wriggled to get free, but he pulled her closer to him. Military training, it seemed, meant that the waltz was his only dance move. Hearing the beat of a faster number,

Alina twisted out of his grip and joined Linda and Fiona. 'Do you need to rescue Ralph again?' whispered Alina in Fiona's ear.

Fiona glanced over at her husband, once again arguing with Kitty Blenkinsop. 'I've told him to let it rest, but he's not listening to me.' She raised the palms of her hands upwards. 'What can I do?'

Fitz came to dance beside them, and Alina gave him a quick smile. 'This is how it's done now-a-days,' she said, despite being very unsure if Claire would approve of her dance moves.

'If you say so, Alina.' The major placed his lips near her ear but still yelled.

Alina hunched her shoulders, covering her ear. She stepped back away from him, and wondered when she could excuse herself. As if her prayers were answered, a slow beat came from the speakers, and Alina slipped off the dance floor and headed towards the toilets. The young waitress she'd seen earlier gave her a brief nod before washing her hands thoroughly and leaving the ladies'.

Returning to the ballroom, Alina collapsed into a chair at a table near the dance floor. Kitty Blenkinsop was slumped in the chair next to her. Clearly she'd managed to rid herself of Ralph Pomeroy.

'You've done well, Kitty. I think we've raised a fortune for the roof. The auction was a great idea.' Alina sat up, frowning at Kitty, not a little miffed at the lack of response.

'Is she ignoring you, Vicar?' Amy Pretty asked. 'She's so rude.' She walked unsteadily past the table, clasping her bag in front of her chest. Her fingertips grazed over the tablecloth, helping her to maintain her balance as she headed towards the ladies' toilets. When she ran out of table to balance against, she turned her head. Eyes bulging, Amy's hand flew to her mouth. She screamed.

'Amy? What's wrong?' Alina jumped to her aching feet to steady the old lady.

'I'm fine, I'm fine,' squealed Amy. 'Look at her face!'

She raised her hand, pointing at Kitty, and Alina leaned in, putting her hand on Kitty's shoulder. Kitty fell to the floor.

'Is she drunk?' said Amy.

'Yes, I think so. It's been quite an evening, hasn't it? I expect we've all overdone it a bit,' said Alina. She dropped to the floor and pressed her fingers into Kitty's neck, feeling for the pulse. Nothing. She pressed harder. Still nothing. She rocked back on her heels and gave Amy a close-lipped smile. 'Amy, can you call an ambulance, please?'

'She's not just drunk, is she? Why does she need an ambulance if she's simply drunk?' Amy's voice rose higher and higher. People dancing turned in their direction. The band fell silent.

'What's going on here, then?' Pushing his way through the crowd, PC Rigg towered over the two women.

Alina pushed herself up from the floor. 'Kitty's dead, Bert,' she said. 'We need an ambulance. A paramedic can pronounce life extinct and time of death.'

'Heart attack?' said Bert.

'I don't think so. I think it may be poisoning,' Alina whispered, tilting her head close to his. 'See her face—the cherry red colouring. And look at her handkerchief. There's a little vomit on it. That could be due to alcohol, which of course is a poison, but I think she would have had time to get to the loo. I think this is something more serious.'

'I'd better call the inspector,' said PC Rigg.

Alina nodded, her mind racing. *What would private eye Judy Jacobs be doing? Collecting possible evidence, of course.* 'And bag up her glass,' said Alina, thinking back to Kitty's arguments with the waitress and Ralph. 'If she was poisoned, that's probably how it was done.'

CHAPTER NINE

Silence on the dance floor evaporated as the whispers began. Gently at first, like a soft wind through the trees, then the commotion rose to a harsh buzz. Soon the room was in uproar.

'Stand back! Stand back!' PC Rigg shouted, his arms held wide to corral the burgeoning crowd.

'What's happened?' one voice hissed. 'Is she drunk?'

'Is she dead?' asked another.

'Good riddance.'

Alina snapped her head around at this last comment. *Who'd said that?* She ran her gaze over all the faces. Uniform shock registered on them all. Yet someone had seen Kitty's death as a relief. Something good. Something beneficial. But who? She scanned the crowd until her eyes rested on the young waitress who stood, hands on hips, a slight smile playing on her lips.

She stayed by Kitty's body—highly aware of the anxious crowd whispering behind her—until the paramedics arrived.

'Hi Geoff,' she said, recognising the man with a bulging green rucksack.

'What have we got here, nurse?' he replied.

Inwardly, Alina smiled at the use of her other title. Most people called her Vicar, but Geoff only knew her through her other profession. 'She was fine earlier, at the dinner and the speeches. We had a charity auction and she ran that. Then we started dancing. I got tired and came to sit down next to her. That would have been around ten thirty. I chatted to her for a while, but she didn't reply. Then Amy walked past on her way to the loo. She noticed something was wrong. Then we called you.'

'Well, she's definitely dead,' said Geoff.

'Thanks for that,' said Alina, with a wry smile. 'I got top marks in diagnosis in my younger days.'

Geoff smiled briefly. 'We'll need a doctor to sign a death certificate—'

'Not so fast.'

Alina looked up at the owner of the voice. He was a tall, slim man, greying at the temples, with a face that wouldn't be unpleasant if he were not glaring at both her and Geoff quite so fiercely.

'I beg your pardon?' Alina pushed herself to her feet, but still had to look up at the man.

'Inspector Laidlaw, this is Alina Merrycott,' interceded Bert Rigg. 'She's our vicar and district nurse.'

'I don't really care who she is since she's trampling all over my crime scene,' replied the inspector.

'Crime scene?' Alina said, rubbing at the goosebumps on her arms.

'It's a sudden death, Miss Merrycott,' Laidlaw said. 'No death certificate will be issued until after the inquest. In the meantime, I'll need to ask you all some questions. Bert, is there another room we can use?'

'You can use my office,' said Ralph Pomeroy, elbowing his

way out of the crowd. 'I'm the men's club captain. I have a little office. Here, I'll show you.'

DI Laidlaw nodded curtly and followed Ralph out of the ballroom.

'Everyone please take your seats,' shouted PC Rigg. 'The inspector and these other officers will need to speak to you all.'

Muttering, the dancers and diners resumed their places at tables. Uniformed officers visited each table, taking names and addresses.

'Bloody woman,' Fiona Pomeroy groused. 'Needed to be the centre of attention in life and is just the same now she's dead.'

'Shush, darling,' said Ralph, as he pulled his chair out and sat down next to his wife. 'Don't speak ill of the dead and all that.'

Fiona glared at him.

Alina leaned back in her chair, staring around the room at her parishioners. Most were in the type of shock that sudden death brings. There was a hum of conversation in the room. No doubt speculation over who could have done such a thing.

'Vicar,' whispered a voice behind her. The gentle breath on her neck made Alina shiver. *When had the room become so hot?* 'The inspector will see you now.'

Alina looked up at the young police officer. Her face was drawn. Perhaps this is her first death, thought Alina. *I wish it were mine.* She followed the officer to the golf-club captain's office.

'Come in, Miss Merrycott. Do sit down.' Inspector Laidlaw chewed the end of his pen and didn't look up as Alina entered the room.

'It's Nurse Merrycott or Reverend Merrycott. Whichever you prefer. And I'm a widow, so not Miss under any circumstances,' said Alina. Still annoyed by his earlier brusque manner, she perched on the edge of the chair, dropping her bag to the floor. Staring disapprovingly at the pen chewing, she folded her arms.

Inspector Laidlaw finally raised his head and looked at her for the first time. Alina returned the stare. Exhaustion dulled his deep brown eyes. *Was it because he was asking the same questions over and over again?*

'So, Reverend Merrycott, where were you when the body was discovered?'

'You know that, Inspector. I was kneeling beside her. I'd just reached over her to feel for her pulse.'

'And before that?' He flipped the pages in his notebook back and forth.

'I was sitting next to her, telling her what a great job she'd done raising money for the church roof.'

'And that's what this event was in aid of?' DI Laidlaw rubbed his forehead, pinching the top of his nose between thumb and forefinger.

'Yes, Inspector. St Edmund's roof needs repairing, just the same as any other roof of any church in the country. Ours has a particularly fine ceiling which needs preserving. Perhaps you've seen it?'

'I don't get time for staring at ceilings,' replied Laidlaw, wrinkling his brow. 'So, back to Mrs Blenkinsop. What can you tell me about her?'

'Not much to be honest,' Alina said. 'She was new to the village. I've been here around nine months. Kitty arrived not long after me.'

'Is she popular with the other villagers?'

'No, I wouldn't say that.' Alina twisted her hands in her

lap. 'Kitty had a way about her which grated. People didn't take to her.'

'How do you mean?' he tapped the biro against his chin.

'Well, it seems she's taken over some of the local clubs and groups. It hasn't gone down well with the incumbents.'

'Enough to kill over?'

Alina thought back over the last two days. Had she seen enough of Kitty's manner to know whether it would get her killed? Yes, the woman was irritating, but sufficiently irritating to kill? 'Hard to say, Inspector. I don't tend to regard my parishioners as potential murderers. I try to see the good in people. I think people will, for the most part, do the right thing.'

Inspector Laidlaw snorted but tried to turn it into a cough. 'You should be in my job,' he said. 'You see the worst of people all the time.'

'Then I'm sorry for you, Inspector,' Alina said. 'Will that be all?'

'No. Not yet,' he replied. 'Did *you* have any reason to dislike her?'

'Me? No, of course not! Why should I have any reason to dislike her, let alone kill her?' Alina rubbed the back of her head. *How on earth has he come up with this crazy idea?*

'Hasn't she got her claws into your major?' Inspector Laidlaw rested his hands on the ink blotter, stretching out his long, slim fingers.

Alina laughed. 'Major Fitzgerald and I are just friends,' she said. 'He's not *my* major at all. I've no idea where you got that notion. It's all nonsense.'

The inspector arched his eyebrows and said. 'Oh, just gossip, you know. I always listen to gossip.'

'Well, Inspector, I never do. Was there anything else you wanted to ask me?'

'I'll need you to make a formal statement, but you can do that at the station.'

Alina pushed her chair away from the desk.

'Tell me,' the inspector said, 'why did you suggest bagging up the glass?'

Looking at her unpolished fingernails, Alina murmured, 'I'm a fan of the Judy Jacobs mysteries.'

'Are those detective stories? Full of bloody interfering amateurs,' DI Laidlaw sneered.

'I'll wish you a good evening, Inspector,' Alina said, rising and collecting her small bag from the floor. She strode from the room, only just resisting the urge to slam the door behind her.

CHAPTER TEN

Alina made her way to the ladies' toilets, stepped into an empty cubicle, and leaned against the door. *What an insufferable man! How dare he suggest I could murder someone.* She relaxed her clenched fists, suddenly realising she could cheerfully murder the inspector right now. She breathed in and released the breath slowly. More calmly, she told herself that it must be very hard having a job when you always saw humanity at its worst. That must be it. She closed her eyes for a moment, then snapped them open. Images of soft deep brown eyes and silvering curls at his temples were not what she needed right now.

She plonked herself down on the toilet seat, allowing her mind to go blank. It was something she'd always found useful, a way to free her mind of stress and intrusive thoughts. Not that she imagined DI Laidlaw intruding on her thoughts too often. She heard other women outside the door, so she completed her business and flushed the loo. She opened the door and stepped out.

'Well, you won't be sorry to see the back of her, will you, Amy?' said Linda Cranford.

Reflected in the mirror, an expression of triumph flashed across Amy's face before she realised Alina was standing behind her.

'No, no, of course not. How can you say such a thing?' Amy hung her head, gripping the basin, her knuckles white. She turned from the basin and pushed past Alina to go into the now empty cubicle. At the sound of the first sob, Linda gave Alina a quick shrug and left the ladies'.

'Amy,' said Alina, biting back her frustration at Linda's callous behaviour. She knocked on the cubicle door. 'Amy, are you okay?'

'Go away,' sniffed Amy.

'I think it would be good to talk,' said Alina. 'I am a good listener.'

On the other side of the door, Alina heard Amy sniff and blow her nose.

'I hated her,' Amy replied. 'It was no secret. If she's been murdered the police will think it's me.'

'At the moment, it's a suspicious death. The police won't know if it's murder until after a post-mortem. Amy, come out here,' said Alina. 'It's very hard to talk through a door.'

Alina took a half-step back as she heard the bolt slide back. 'You know I hated her. I told you as much this morning.' Amy sniffed again, and Alina's stomach recoiled thinking of the lace handkerchief.

Please God, let it be a clean one, she thought. The handkerchief was a crisp linen with an embroidered monogram. Alina sighed with relief. 'I know you were upset,' Alina said. 'You told me how much the shop means to you and your retirement plans. That's all.'

'What did you tell the police?' Amy's normally watery eyes took on a sharp expression.

'About you? Nothing,' said Alina. 'They didn't ask about

you. They didn't ask about anyone. If anything, I think that inspector might suspect me.'

'You? Why you?' Amy frowned.

'Because Kitty grabbed the major after arguing with Ralph Pomeroy. Inspector Laidlaw thinks that Kitty was stealing him away from me.'

'I didn't realise you and the major were so close.'

'Nor did I,' replied Alina with a wry smile. 'So you see, you're not the only person DI Laidlaw's got his eye on. Just tell him the truth and it will all be fine.'

'If you say so,' Amy mumbled.

The two women jumped at a sharp rap on the door.

'Are you in there, Vicar?' shouted the major. 'We can go if you're ready.'

'Will you be okay?' Alina squeezed Amy's hands.

'Yes, I'll be fine,' she said. 'I've got a lift with Mrs Rigg. She'll drive me back. She said Bert will get a lift home in one of the police cars later.'

'Good,' said Alina. 'I'll see you in the morning.' Although, she thought, looking at her watch, it already was Sunday morning.

Alina strolled down the front steps of the golf club. Major Fitzgerald stood by the car, his hand on the top of the open passenger door. Alina slid her bottom against the car's body, glad that it was clean. She'd experienced enough of the major's wandering hands whilst they were dancing. It wasn't something she wanted to continue. Slipping into the passenger seat, she covered her knees as best she could with the dress and tiny handbag.

'Did they grill you too?' asked Fitz, as he jumped into the driver's seat and pulled away.

'A little,' said Alina. 'They wanted to know more about you and Mrs Blenkinsop, to be honest.'

'Me? Why me?' Fitz snorted with derision.

'Apparently she was stealing you away from me.' Alina bit her tongue. Perhaps now wasn't the time to broach the subject. She held her breath, waiting for a reply. The major drove along in silence.

'She could never have done that, Alina,' he said finally. 'I value my friends. That's not something Kitty could have ever understood.'

'Why do you say that?' said Alina.

'Simple. She didn't have any friends. You saw what she was like. Bossing everyone around. Stomping on everyone. Look how badly she treated Ralph this evening. All she had to say was that there was no top table, but she insulted him by saying he simply wasn't on the top table.'

'She could have been more gracious,' said Alina carefully.

'That's a very polite way of putting it,' said the major. 'But she wasn't getting me away from you, old girl.' Fitz patted her knee and gave it a little squeeze.

'Major... Fitz...' Alina began.

'Oh I know. You're still in your widow's weeds,' he said. 'I can wait. I can be patient.'

Alina sighed, wondering how she could let him down gently. She'd agreed with the bishop that she would call herself a widow and, since she'd had Jake declared dead, technically she was. If he were ever to come back into her life, he'd have no claim over her. But over Claire? A claim over her lovely daughter? Biting her lip, she thought back to recent conversations with Claire. *Why does she think her father is still alive? Has she heard from him?* Alina knew she'd have to discuss Jake with Claire the next time she was home, but it could wait for now. After all, they had delayed the conversation for several years.

Her thoughts returning once more to her missing husband, she shook her head. *Who are you kidding,* she asked herself. *He still has a claim over you. Over your heart.* Blinking the tears away, she stared out at the dark countryside, wondering what had happened to him between their little house in Bournemouth and the shop on the corner where he'd gone to buy some milk. Blast! she thought. What a cliché! But he didn't come back, and after a while she realised that he never would.

CHAPTER ELEVEN

Thalia was curled up on the hearth rug in front of the glowing embers of the dying fire, with the tip of her tail covering her nose, when Alina entered her cottage. She rolled onto her back, stretched out her legs and then relaxed, her body limp, although staring at Alina intently. Alina dropped to her knees by the cat and stroked the available belly fur. As she did so, her pulse slowed and her mind stopped racing.

'I still can't believe it,' she told the cat. 'She dropped dead right beside me. There was nothing I could do.'

'Meow,' said Thalia and she rose to snuggle herself on what lap was available.

'Oh no, not on a black dress, puddy-tat,' Alina said, but she looked down at the garment's short skirt and decided it didn't matter. She was unlikely to wear this dress ever again. Alina scooped Thalia up and they sat on the sofa together, Alina's thoughts of the evening's events chasing through her head. Then one thought stuck. *I'm going to have to redo my sermon.* She looked at the clock on the mantelshelf over the fire. One o'clock in the morning. Sunday morning! Running the numbers in her head, Alina worked out that if she slept through until nine in the morning she could get at least a few hours' sleep.

Placing the cat on a cushion, she strolled to the kitchen, made herself a cup of herbal tea, put another log on the sitting room fire and settled down with her notepad, bible and pen.

Turning to James chapter four again, she read the second verse:

You want something and you do not have it;
so you commit murder.
And you covet...

Murder, she whispered. *Is that really what happened?* It was unlikely to be natural causes, she knew only too well. She'd never seen Kitty at the doctors' surgery, although she could probably find out if there had been any underlying heart problems. The handkerchief worried her. The specks of vomit and a hint of almonds. *Or did I imagine the smell?* Shaking her head, she took a sip of tea and admonished herself for turning into Miss Marple. 'You're not even that good at knitting,' she muttered, looking guiltily at the basket with knitting needles and the bag of yarn she'd bought that morning poking out the top.

'Sermon,' she muttered. 'Focus.' Still new to her ministerial profession, she drafted an email to her supervisor for guidance on her mobile phone. The format for a funeral service was laid out in the Book of Common Prayer, but that would be later, after the post-mortem, possibly even after the inquest. Kitty was a widow. Childless. Who was her next of kin? Would her next of kin even want Kitty laid to rest in Eastwold? What arrangements had Kitty made? Had she even considered her mortality? Question after question raced through Alina's head. She buried her face in Thalia's fluffy coat. Focus on one thing at a time, she thought. *What am I going to preach about tomorrow?* She opened her eyes and lifted her head. Two faces swum into her head. Neither one was Kitty, the person she should be thinking about. She snapped her eyes open, sipped more of the cooling tea, and laid her hand on her Bible. After a moment she picked it up and opened it randomly, pleading for guidance. Paul's first letter to the Corinthians; the gift of love. She completed the email and hoped for an answer before the morning service.

Holding Thalia up, she smiled at the grumpy-looking creature. 'I'm going to bed now,' she said. 'Where do you want to be?'

As a reply, Thalia wriggled free and curled herself up on the hearth rug once more. 'Very well,' said Alina, and she prodded at the glowing log, replaced the fireguard, and headed for bed.

After a restless night's sleep, Alina decided to cycle to church, hoping that the fresh air would perk her up. Jumbled thoughts ran through her head. The disagreements of the previous few days over flowers and seating. Her medical training led her to believe that the death was unnatural, although she knew she'd have to wait for the post-mortem results to be sure. She dismounted at the church gate and wheeled the bicycle to the side door, knowing it would be safe. It was a rickety old thing in any case. Who would want it? She pushed down the heavy latch and, shoulder to the door, heaved it open.

'Oh Vicar, what a terrible thing to happen. I've hardly slept a wink!' Joanne looked flustered. She was only half-robed, and her short dark hair was uncombed as she flapped around the small vestry.

'I know how you feel, Jo,' replied Alina. 'Any chance of a coffee before I go on?'

'Oh Vicar, you do make me laugh. You make it sound like you're going on stage, like Madonna,' Joanne twittered. 'Let me get you one now. Biscuit?'

Alina thought back to her single slice of toast for breakfast and nodded. Pulling open the wardrobe, she selected her vestments for the day, removing the white stole from Friday's wedding. Was it only Friday that everyone had been so happy? It seemed such a very long time ago. Replacing it with a green stole for summer services and ensuring the index cards with her scant notes were easy to reach, she risked a peek into the church to see how many had turned up. There was usually a reasonable turnout in summer. The church often got close to a third full. She gasped. It was packed. *How has news got around so quickly?* English villages and small towns. She smiled to herself. There seemed little need for the high-speed fibre broadband being installed in Eastwold when the gossip machine was clearly hard at work.

'Your coffee, Vicar.'

'Thank you,' Alina said automatically, regarding the muddy-coloured liquid with dismay. She smiled at the anxious woman, took a sip, and smiled. 'Lovely,' she said. 'Just what I needed.' She tiptoed back to the vestry, hoping that the biscuits would make up for the watery coffee, to be met by two dull-looking Rich Tea biscuits. She prodded at them. They were stale.

She pulled her shoulders back and, raising her chin, she prepared herself mentally for the service. Although never a shy person, Alina still found it a little intimidating to stand in front of a group of people to talk. She was getting better – practice makes for improvement, she thought.

Raising her hands to ask the congregation to stand, she saw Richard Laidlaw in the third row. His attire was similar to what he'd worn the previous night with the simple addition of a tie. Catching her eye, he smiled, and

Alina wondered if he was a regular attendee or if he was simply trying to catch a killer. She shivered unexpectedly, but told herself it was just a chilly draught, only to be expected in such an old building. Then she nodded and said, 'Our first hymn will be *Praise my Soul the King of Heaven*.'

Alina sat too long as the words of the gospel reading faded away. Fitz came to sit beside her in the old choir pews. 'Come on,' he said.

Alina stared at him. For a moment she'd forgotten where she was. She rose and dragged herself into the pulpit. She gazed at the index cards clutched in her hands and then raised her gaze to the congregation.

'I had planned to talk about the seven deadly sins today. I'd even narrowed it down to one sin in particular,' she hesitated, 'but in the light of last night's events, I've chosen to talk about St Paul's first letter to the Corinthian church and, in particular, the gift of love.'

She stared at the expectant faces—was that why DI Laidlaw was here? To see all the suspects in one place? Unusually, everyone was here, with only a few exceptions. The young waitress from the previous evening, who she'd discovered was called Tracy Goring, was a new face in the pews. Joanne had told her that Tracy's three children were in Sunday school.

'Love is patient, love is kind,' she intoned. She raised her head to see the impact of her words on Linda Cranford, Ralph and Fiona Pomeroy, Amy Pretty and the young waitress, Tracy Goring. They all stared back at her, with the exception of Tracy, who was fidgeting, biting her fingernails, and staring towards the windows looking as if she wished she could escape through them.

'And now faith, hope and love abide—and the greatest of these is love. Blessed be the name of the Lord.'

Alina allowed silence to hang for a moment. She looked down, gripping the edge of the lectern. Richard was staring at her intently, with a faint smile playing around his lips. Alina blinked rapidly, trying to raise the image of his lips from her mind. She dropped her hand and pinched her thigh through the surplice. *Get a grip, get a grip.* Aloud she said, 'Let us pray.'

Fitz lurked at the back of the church until Alina had said goodbye to the last parishioner. If he was trying to make DI Laidlaw, or anyone else for that matter, believe there was nothing between them, he was doing a very poor job.

'I thought you'd be heading for the pub with Wilf as usual,' she said.

'I wanted a chat after last night. Make sure you were tickety boo,' he replied, concern etched across his lined face.

'I'm as well as can be expected for a murder suspect,' Alina replied. Did I really say that out loud, she wondered. I can't believe this is happening again. 'Did you notice fewer people wanted to shake my hand today?'

'Can't say I noticed. Has he told you you're a suspect?' asked Fitz.

'Not in so many words, I grant you, but I was the one to find her. I was the one leaning over her body. However you look at it, it's not good.'

'Come and have a drink. Take your mind off things,' Fitz said.

'I can't,' said Alina. 'I have to call the bishop at home this afternoon. He wants me to give him a "heads up", as he called it. Then I suppose I'll have to do the same at the surgery tomorrow.'

'Very well, old girl,' replied Fitz. 'You know where I am if you need the old shoulder. I've plenty of tissues.'

Alina gave him a faint smile. He tipped his Sunday best hat and sauntered to the St Edmund's Arms. Alina turned around and made her way back to the vestry to change into her street clothes.

CHAPTER TWELVE

The surgery was one of the few really modern buildings in Eastwold. Alina often puzzled over how it got planning permission in a town that prided itself on aesthetics, but it was purpose-built for an ageing population. She pressed her identity card against the electronic pad, and the glass doors clicked and slid back to allow her to enter. Even so, she always felt she needed to dive like an injured footballer to get over the threshold before the doors slid shut again. At least they're less aggressive when the surgery is open for patients, Alina thought. Elderly and wheelchair bound patients would be constantly squished between the panels of glass and metal otherwise.

The hum of conversation stopped as soon as she entered the reception area. Ros Cauthorn, the practice manager, raised her head to look Alina up and down before saying, 'A word! In my office, if you don't mind, Nurse Merrycott.'

Alina winked at Seda Magnat, the receptionist. 'Am I in some sort of trouble, Ros?' she asked, closing the door behind her. She half-wondered if the rest of the staff had abandoned reception to come and listen at the thin door. She checked for shadows just in case. There were none.

'I wanted to hear the full story of your involvement in the death of one of our patients. Dr McCarthy will be in shortly and I shall need to give her your full version of events,' Ros replied.

'Won't it be easier if I do that?' Alina said. She smiled, tilting her head to one side. It diffused the situation with most people, but for some reason it always riled Ros Cauthorn. Alina had no idea why it annoyed her, but since she'd never taken to the pompous practice manager, she found herself doing it much more frequently.

'I need to know what happened,' snapped Ros. She pulled her glasses from her face, and squinted at Alina. 'In case the police ask me.'

'Are they likely to do that? I didn't realise you were at the ball too. Did you have a good time?' Alina wondered why she didn't keep the glasses on if she needed to peer so.

'No, I wasn't at the ball. Couldn't get a ticket. That ghastly Blenkinsop woman wouldn't sell me one,' Ros complained. She rammed the glasses back on her nose, leaving a smear on one lens. 'Now, what happened?'

'I'm sorry, but I'm still under strict instructions from the police not to share my "version of events", as you call it. I have been told that I can, of course, share in confidence with my employer. That's Dr McCarthy. But I can't share with you or with anyone else.'

'I've never heard anything so ridiculous in all my life,' snorted Ros. She stood and stormed out of the room, slamming the door behind her.

I wonder if she's forgotten it's her office? Alina rubbed her hands over her face and yawned. What a weekend! She didn't think she'd ever catch up on her sleep. Standing and leaving the hard chair behind, she strolled back to reception. Seda had a steaming hot cup of coffee waiting for her.

'So, spill, what happened?' Seda said.

Alina didn't fail to notice that Seda was maintaining a tight hold on the biscuit barrel. *Is bribery to be involved?* 'I've told Ros, I can't say anything.'

'Is that the truth?' Seda frowned. Her hazel eyes sparkled and her grasp on the biscuit barrel loosened.

'It is. I'm a vicar. I'm not allowed to lie,' Alina said. 'Mrs Blenkinsop didn't have any heart problems, did she?'

'You know I can't tell you that,' said Seda. Her voice rose an octave. 'Patient confidentiality! She wasn't a patient of yours, was she?'

Alina shook her head and sipped more coffee. Seda slid the biscuit tin towards her as a peace offering, but Alina found she'd lost her appetite.

'How are you, Alina?' said Dr Miriam McCarthy as she ushered Alina into her consulting room. 'It must have been a terrible shock.' The doctor pushed her wire-rimmed spectacles further up her nose. Concern washed over her face, amplified in her cornflower blue eyes.

'We're trained to expect death, aren't we?' said Alina. 'But yes, it was a shock when she fell off the chair beside me. I'd hoped she was simply drunk. But a part of me sensed she'd gone even before I searched for a pulse. Have the police been in touch?'

'Yes, I had a call yesterday from a...' — Dr McCarthy peered at her mobile phone — 'Inspector Richard Laidlaw. Is he as dishy as his voice sounds?'

Alina frowned. *Was he?* 'He's not unpleasant looking,' she finally conceded. 'He was very stern with me.'

'Are you a suspect?'

'No, not at the moment,' sighed Alina. 'I had a long call with the bishop yesterday. He's rather anxious in case I am charged…' Alina spread her palms upwards, shrugging slightly.

'Oh dear,' said Dr McCarthy. 'Well, let's wait for the outcome of the autopsy and see where we are then. Dealing with people's illnesses in their own homes requires a lot of trust, and if you're under the slightest suspicion—' Dr McCarthy shrugged. 'I'm sure I don't need to say anything more, do I?'

'No,' replied Alina. She'd been incredibly lucky to get the two jobs within weeks of each other. Getting Claire out of London was the entire reason for moving to Eastwold, but now it could all be snatched away. 'When is the autopsy?'

'DI Laidlaw said it would be tomorrow afternoon. He wanted to know if Mrs Blenkinsop had any underlying heart conditions.' Dr McCarthy logged onto her computer, bringing up patient records. 'But it doesn't look like it. Overweight, obviously. Fit as a flea otherwise.' She removed her glasses and used the arms to scratch her head. She smoothed down the shaggy blonde curls and rested her hands in her lap. 'And you're sure you're okay?'

'Yes. It was a bit of a shock, but I'm fine now. Did the inspector say when he'd know the cause of death?'

'Yes, in a few days' time. He thinks the inquest will be next week.'

Alina nodded. A sudden death was always followed by an inquest, to ascertain if the cause of the demise was a natural one or not. If not, Alina knew that an investigation would be opened. However, it seemed that even without the post-mortem results, Inspector Laidlaw was investigating already. She snapped out of her reverie, realising that Miriam McCarthy was asking a question.

'Sorry, I was thinking about Kitty,' she said. 'I missed that.'

'Mr Mahoney. You're going to see him again today?'

'Yes, after lunch. The wound sites are healing well but I'm sure he's not taking the medication, so he's likely to have another flare-up.'

'Remind him that it'll lead to long-term problems and that he may become housebound if he continues with his current diet.'

Alina nodded, reflecting how tricky it would be to get on the right side of the curmudgeonly Cedric Mahoney.

'Can you put in a call to Tracy Goring? She's worried about her youngest. It doesn't sound serious, but Kriya asked if you could drop by.'

Alina smiled. Kriya Andhra was the latest addition to the team. A social worker, originally from Birmingham, she had a sharp eye and was well attuned to problems caused by living on the poverty line. Eastwold was a mostly prosperous town but, like every town in the British Isles, it had families who dropped off the radar.

Walking to her car, she decided to call Kriya and see what she'd spotted.

'Kriya, Alina Merrycott here.'

'Ah, Alina, thank you for calling. I'm very concerned about Tracy Goring. She left me a message. Her youngest isn't well. Can you go and see her?' Kriya's soft voice gave little away about her background, although the Birmingham accent slipped through.

'Of course, I've put her top of my list. Then I'll go and see Cedric Mahoney. Have you been able to sort a home help for him yet?'

'No, he's still not keen on the idea, but I'm with you. The whole house is a mess. Have you seen upstairs?'

'Er, no,' said Alina. 'I've not needed to go up there.'

'Don't! It's dangerous. Piles and piles of rubbish and old newspapers. It's a fire hazard.'

'At least he won't be going up there for a while,' replied Alina. 'Do you want me to ask around whilst I'm on my travels?'

'Could you? You're an angel.'

'Not quite,' laughed Alina. 'But we may find some kind soul. Anyway, I'd better go and see Ms Goring and her little boy. Shall I give you an update later?'

'That would be lovely, thanks Alina.'

CHAPTER THIRTEEN

Alina placed her medical bag onto Delia's back seat and hopped into the front. She murmured a short prayer as she turned the ignition key, and Delia reluctantly rumbled into life. Checking her list of visits for Tracy's address, she slipped the car into gear and chugged up the road, out of town and away from the sea.

Norton Road faced a salt marsh. Flat open ground, often flooded during the winter, it was still considered by some as a prime development site. So far, Eastwold Council had rejected all offers to buy and develop the land, but Alina wondered how much longer the council could hold the developers at bay.

Number thirty-eight was a small, red-brick, mid-terraced cottage. The upper half was rendered and painted a pale cream. It needed a fresh coat but, even if Tracy had the money for paint, there was no one to help her. Alina knew what it was like to be a single mother. She'd raised Claire on her own after Jake hadn't returned from the corner shop. But at least she had a job, family support and only one child to worry about. Tracy had rather more on her plate.

Alina rang the doorbell, noticing the cobwebs in the tiny porch and the leaves blown into the porchway from last autumn's winds. She rang again, and was surprised to hear the yapping of a small dog. Its nose thrust through the gap when the front door was finally wrenched open.

Tracy Goring's appearance had altered dramatically from Saturday night—lack of sleep and worry had rendered the young woman waif-like, and her light brown hair was scraped off her face in a style known as the Coventry face lift. Dark circles under her eyes stretched as far as her cheekbones, which jutted out as sharply as the groynes on the beach. 'At long last. I'm going out of my mind here!' All this was shouted as the petite woman tried to lever the door open whilst pushing the yapping terrier back inside the house.

'I didn't know you'd got a dog, Tracy,' said Alina, trying to force a cheery tone into her voice. She looked suspiciously at the dog, who was sniffing around her feet.

'I in't. It's me mum's. She's been in hospital since her stroke and I got lumbered with 'im. Come through, Ethan's in 'ere.'

Alina followed the young woman down the tight hallway to the front room. Ethan was lying on the sofa under a tatty baby blanket. He was pale and breathing rapidly. Alina touched his forehead. The child was burning up. She reached into her medical bag and took the child thermometer out and placed it on his forehead while she felt his hands and feet. Chilled. 'Has he been sick?' she asked.

Tracy nodded. 'Up all night I was with 'im. I've sent the others off to school. It's hard coping on me own since Dave left.'

'Yes, I know,' murmured Alina. 'Could you bring me a glass?'

'Yeah, what you want? Squash? Water? I was gonna make you a coffee,' said Tracy.

'No, just the glass, please. No water or anything.'

'Right you are.' Tracy gazed at her son before she left the room, her harsh features softening.

A mother's love, thought Alina. She took her torch out of the bag and flashed it against the child's eyes. He squinted and whimpered at the brightness.

Tracy quickly returned, handing Alina the glass, and she slid the boy's pyjama trouser leg up to his knee. The red spots she'd seen on his feet were more prevalent here, and she pressed the glass against the spots on the boy's calf.

'Blast,' she whispered to herself. Taking her mobile out of her pocket, she dialled 999. 'Ambulance please,' she said.

Tracy screamed and collapsed to the floor, hugging the terrier close to her. 'What is it?' she cried.

'It could be meningitis,' Alina replied. 'I'd like to get him into hospital for tests. The others are at school, you said?'

'Yeah,' said Tracy, wiping her nose on the dog's coat.

While they waited, Tracy's wails outdid those of the ambulance, and Alina jumped at the banging of fists on the door. She rushed down the corridor to open the door.

'You again,' said Geoff. 'What we got?'

'Suspected meningitis,' Alina replied.

Geoff pushed his way into the front room, making the room look even smaller than it had. He flashed a torch across the boy's eyes, removed the sticky temperature strip, read it, and scooped the child up into his arms. 'Get me a blanket!' he shouted to Mandy, his colleague.

She came back with a dark green blanket, the same colour as her uniform. Geoff wrapped the small boy in it as tenderly as if the boy were a new-born.

'You're driving,' he said to Mandy. 'We leave now,' he said to Tracy, who dropped the dog to the floor. She grabbed her handbag and raced out of the house, trying to keep pace with the man holding her child.

Alina regarded the dog, who sat on the floor thumping his small tail against the floor. 'Let's hope she's got her keys with her,' said Alina. She closed the front door and shooed the dog into the kitchen. She let him in the garden for a while as she made sure he had water and put some kibble into a bowl for him. That done, she phoned the surgery. 'Seda, do we know what school the other Goring children go to? Good. Can you call them and let them know what's happened. Mum has gone to the hospital, so there's no one to look after them, but we should take precautions against the spread.'

Taking one last look around the house, and hoping that Tracy had her keys with her, Alina closed the front door and walked towards the pavement. She whispered a prayer for Ethan's rapid recovery.

'Hey, what's happened?'

Alina turned sharply. The speaker was an elderly lady with bright brown eyes—small and glittering like a bear's.

'Well?' The old woman leaned heavily on her walking frame.

'The little one has been taken to hospital,' Alina replied. 'Are you a friend of the family?'

'I sit for her sometimes,' said the old woman. 'She's a good girl is Tracy. Works hard. Not easy on her own.'

'No, it's not,' said Alina. Turning to her car, a sudden thought struck. 'Were you looking after the children on Saturday night?'

'I was. What's it to you?'

'The little one has been taken sick. Very sick. You might want to make an appointment to see your GP. Soon.'

The old woman nodded. 'That poor girl's got enough on her plate. She doesn't need any more trouble, bless her.' Shuffling back inside her house, she flicked aside her net curtains to get a clear view. She was still watching as Alina drove away. No need for a watchdog with her around.

Heading back towards the cliff top and Cedric's home, Alina thought about Kitty Blenkinsop. She'd not known the woman well, despite a number of attempts to draw her into conversation. As far as she knew, Kitty was only interested in people's lives when she sensed there was a secret. Although Alina knew she was lonely, she was at least beginning to make friends. Kitty, it seemed, had no one.

Alina parked in the row of cars near Cedric's home. The Meals on Wheels van was parked close by, and Linda Cranford was coming out of one of the houses near Cedric's. Alina waved, but Linda must not have seen her as she didn't wave back.

Retrieving Cedric's key from the Master Lock, Alina let herself in. Cedric glowered at her when he saw her in the doorway.

'I hope you've not come to kill me too, Nurse,' he said.

'Whatever gave you that idea?' Alina said, as she placed her medical bag on the sofa.

'I heard what you did to that old bat Blenkinsop. Poison, wasn't it?' Cedric grinned maliciously, his lips drawn back to reveal long, yellowed teeth. 'How'd you do it? Poison dart to her throat?'

'I think you've been watching too much television and listening to gossip,' replied Alina. 'I found her body, so I'm being questioned by the police the same as everyone else who was there that night.'

'A little birdie tells me they questioned you more than anyone else. You was in with the inspector much longer than her from Meals on Wheels, for instance.'

'Ah, so that's where you've been getting your information,' Alina laughed. 'I don't think he spent any more time with me than he did anyone else.'

At least that explained Linda's behaviour. *I wonder how many other people will think the same?*

'I was sitting next to Kitty before she fell off her chair. She was probably dead before I sat down. I felt for her pulse. I wasn't digging anything into her throat—poisoned or not. In fact, since the results of the autopsy haven't come back yet, we don't know what the cause of death was.' Alina glared at the old man. 'Now, are you going to let me look at your feet today?'

'Not likely. There's no telling what you'll do. You might want to bump me off for an inheritance, like that Dr Shiphams.'

Alina sighed. 'He was called Dr Shipman,' she said. 'And tell me, have you put me in your will?'

'No, I in't,' said the old man. 'And I in't gonna neither.'

'Well, if I'm not in your will, I have no reason to kill you, do I?' Alina put her hands on her hips. The conversation was getting more ludicrous by the minute.

'You might do it outta spite.' Cedric picked up his walking stick and waved it around as if it were a sword.

'Give me strength,' Alina muttered. 'Mr Mahoney, not only am I nurse but I am also a vicar. I'm not in the habit of killing people.'

'Have you ever lost a patient?' Cedric placed the walking stick between his knees.

'Not due to my negligence or intentional harm,' retorted

Alina. 'But I can see you're upset, so I'll come back another day, when you're feeling calmer.'

Alina picked up her bag and walked out the house. She put a call into the surgery and told the receptionist what had just happened.

CHAPTER FOURTEEN

The second Tuesday evening of the month was, as usual in Eastwold, a meeting of the Eastwold Women's Guild. Even the death of the current president, it appeared, was insufficient grounds to cancel a meeting. Alina had learnt some of the Guild's history—it had sprung into being during the First World War and was a place for town women and countrywomen to come together and learn crafts and skills from each other. As the Guild was non-sectarian, Alina decided to wear jeans and a light jumper over a T-shirt. Tonight, she was going to be learning quilting. Needlework was not one of her strong points and, although she was nervous about demonstrating her lack of skill to the ladies of the Guild, it was a good place to learn all the local news—she refused to call it gossip—and meet people who were non-churchgoers.

As Alina pushed open the door of the village hall, the light buzz of conversation ceased and every woman in the room turned to face her.

Amy Pretty bustled towards her. 'Oh, Vicar,' she said.

'How lovely of you to come. Let me sit you with someone who can show you what we do.'

'Thank you,' said Alina. 'I'm not very good at needlework, but I thought it was a good chance to learn.'

'Of course,' said Amy. 'Well, we're all very friendly here.'

'Those don't look terribly friendly,' said Alina, eyeing the long pins sticking out of the pad attached to Amy's wrist.

'Quilting pins,' said Amy. 'They need to be long to go through the quilt top—that's what we call the decorative part —the wadding and the backing material.'

Alina gave her a wan smile, deciding to keep well away from the vicious-looking pins. 'Sit here,' she said, placing Alina amongst a group of women she knew only slightly from seeing them around Eastwold. Across the table she caught sight of Linda Cranford, who stared briefly and then bowed her head to her needlework. *What* have *I done to upset her?* On Alina's left sat Fiona Pomeroy, and her deft fingers flew across the two edges of material. Perfectly spaced, minute stitches appeared as if by magic. Alina stared, until the hands stopped and the two women gazed at each other. Alina, embarrassed, looked away. On her other side was a young schoolteacher who Alina recognised, but whose name she'd not been told.

'What do you need to know?' said Fiona Pomeroy. 'Have you done quilting before?'

'No,' said Alina. 'It was the one topic where I was something of a dunce at school.'

'Well, I hope you're better a nurse than you are a seamstress,' said the young woman on her right. 'I'm Alice Gifford. I teach at the primary school. I was hoping you could give us all an update on little Ethan Goring. Everybody's been very worried about him.'

Alina took in the young teacher's wide eyes and earnest expression. She's what mother would have called a bluestocking. Alina smiled. 'We caught it quickly. There's every chance he'll make a full recovery. I was going to pop into the hospital later this week and see how he's doing.'

Alice nodded and whispered, 'Thank you.'

At the far end of the table, an older woman with tightly permed curls tutted in a disapproving manner. 'That's all you can expect when the child is being brought up by a single mother.'

'I hardly think meningitis is something caused by his mother's marital status,' Alina said mildly. 'From what I could see, she seemed a very loving mother.'

'Loving,' the woman snorted. 'I suppose that's one word for it.'

'Connie Wheeler,' said Amy in a low voice, 'Don't you dare start spreading gossip again.'

'Gossip? It's not gossip when it's common knowledge,' replied Connie, pursing her thin lips.

'Now then, Connie, that's enough,' said Amy. 'Alina, why don't you sit here? This is a block that Kitty was working on. I wonder if you'd mind taking over from her?'

'Of course not. I'd be happy to help out where I can,' said Alina, pulling her chair closer to the table and picking up the scraps of material. Lumpy uneven stitches met her astonished gaze. Amy had said Kitty was no quilter, but she had expected more than this. It was no wonder Amy was annoyed at being usurped by Kitty Blenkinsop.

'I'd pick it all apart and start again if I were you, Vicar.' Fiona leaned over and passed Alina a seam ripper. 'Careful with these, they can rip through the fabric.'

Alina took the plastic cap off the head of the seam ripper and placed it on the base. It was a nasty looking little instrument with a sharp point, another point covered with a bead, and a vicious-looking blade in the middle.

'Do you know how to use one?' Fiona smiled.

'Yes, undoing stitches was the one thing I excelled at in sewing classes,' said Alina. The women around her tittered. Smiling and nodding their heads over their own work.

'What are you making the quilts for?' Alina asked, after a few moments diligently undoing all of Kitty's work.

'The local hospice,' said Amy. 'It just adds a splash of colour in dark days.'

'Not that Kitty approved,' snorted Connie. 'She wanted us to sell them. Raise money for the church roof. Or at least that's what she said.'

'I can't see a problem with that,' said Alina. She hoped her answer would prompt more conversation about Kitty. 'Was she a good seamstress?'

Connie stared at Alina over her lowered glasses. 'You're sitting there undoing her work. I think you already know the answer to that. Kitty's forte lays elsewhere. Stealing husbands and spreading malicious lies.'

Fiona Pomeroy squealed in pain and Alina darted a look in her direction. The sewing needle had jabbed into Fiona's left index finger and blood was seeping through onto the quilted block she'd been sewing. As the blood spread, Amy reached forward towards Fiona's wounded finger, snatching her handkerchief from its home in her sleeve.

Alina gulped and pulled Fiona to her feet. 'Kitchen,' she said. 'There must be a first aid box.' Pushing Fiona ahead of her, Alina propelled the injured woman towards the kitchen cupboard with a green cross. She hoped it would contain all she needed. She'd left her medical bag and her car at Lighthouse Cottage.

'What happened?' asked Alina, opening the first aid box and selecting the items she needed. 'This is going to hurt.' Bending over her patient's hand, Alina pulled the needle out of Fiona's finger and quickly placed a compress of absorbent material over the wound. The sections of quilted cotton fell to the floor, and Amy picked them up, twittering helplessly.

'Throw it away,' said Fiona. 'I can soon sew some more.'

'But such a waste,' said Amy. She held the needlework away from her body, flapping uselessly as she tried to avoid coming into contact with the blood.

'Are you all right there, Amy?' asked Alina.

'It's just the blood,' said Amy. 'I hate the sight of blood.'

'You get used to it,' said Alina grimly. 'It's heights for me. I can't stand heights. When I first went into the ministry, I even had problems standing in the pulpit, but I was able to overcome it.'

Fiona and Amy broke out into gentle laughter. 'It's true,' said Alina. 'It was very embarrassing, especially when I fainted and fell down the pulpit steps.'

'How did you conquer it?' asked Fiona. Now that the needle was removed from her finger and blood had stopped flowing from the wound, colour had returned to her cheeks.

'Therapy,' said Alina. 'Just some cognitive behavioural therapy.'

Amy nodded and wandered back into the hall.

'You want to tell me what happened in there?' said Alina.

Fiona shook her head, her gaze fixated on the plaster. 'It's all just malicious gossip,' she said. 'Kitty loved to stir things up, although increasingly she was the subject of rumours. She was getting a reputation for stealing husbands. That's why I think she started the chatter about Tracy and Ralph. Tracy used to work for me as a Saturday girl when she was younger. Everyone thought Ralph had his eye on her. But, despite everything everyone says about her, Tracy is a nice girl.'

'So what happened?' asked Alina. Cedric Mahoney's remarks about stolen husbands, especially Linda Cranford's, echoed in her head.

'Tracy took over from Amy as golf club secretary, then she became pregnant.' Fiona bit her lip, raised her head, and stared at the ceiling. She sighed. 'Everyone thought the baby was Ralph's. Clearly they still do. Her boyfriend believed the rumours and left. Ralph denied everything. Tracy even offered to have a paternity test done on the baby. At that point I realised she had not slept with my husband. I've known her since she was fifteen and she's never lied to me.'

'But what about the rest of the town?' asked Alina.

'They can think what they want.' Fiona stood, pushing the kitchen chair away and causing it to clatter against the cupboard door. Through the hatch, Alina saw heads rise and turn towards them, like startled gophers.

Alina began packing away the plasters and unused alcohol wipes. Everything else she placed in the kitchen bin. As a thought occurred, she licked her lips to moisten them before asking, 'Where did Kitty fit in?'

Fiona pursed her lips, her eyes narrowing. 'That old bat just wanted to dig everything up again. She found out about the rumour and decided she could make a little money from it.'

Alina frowned. 'Blackmail?'

'Exactly,' said Fiona. 'Good old-fashioned blackmail. She said she had proof. I didn't believe it and I laughed in her face. But it didn't stop her threatening to tell the entire town that they'd been right all along.'

'I can't believe it,' said Alina.

'Believe what you want, Vicar,' said Fiona. 'That's all Kitty Blenkinsop was. A dirty blackmailer. The world is much better off without her.'

CHAPTER FIFTEEN

Alina groaned at the sound of a knock on her front door on Friday evening. She looked at the dish of Mrs Sullivan's infamous chicken curry she was about to place in the oven, then gave it a quick stir before popping the casserole lid back on, placing everything onto a tray and shoving it in the oven. Brushing her fingers through her hair, she marched to the front door, stopping only briefly to check her reflection in the mirror.

Using the peephole, she fixed a smile on her face before opening the door. 'Inspector, what can I do for you?'

'I've had the initial post-mortem results…' he began.

'And you've come to arrest me?' she quipped.

He grinned, and the lines around his twinkling eyes deepened. 'No, not quite, but I would like to ask you some more questions. I know it's late…' DI Laidlaw took a small step forward.

'Don't worry, it's not that late. I was just preparing supper for me and my daughter. It'll keep. Would you like a drink?' She opened the door and strolled to the back of the house, picking up the red wine from the kitchen table and waving the bottle at him. The inspector followed and she noticed him staring around her cosy kitchen.

'Very nice,' he said. 'But I'm on duty.'

'Tea? Coffee?' she said, approaching the kettle.

'Coffee, thanks. It's going to be a long night.'

'You said you had the results?' Alina said, taking a garishly painted mug from the cupboard over the kettle; primary coloured beach huts fought for space with large seagulls and the Eastwold lighthouse.

'Preliminary results,' he corrected her. 'I shouldn't be telling you this, but it wasn't natural causes.'

'Did you ever think it was?' Alina wondered why he was giving her information on the case. *Am I no longer a suspect?*

'No, and I rather gather you didn't either?'

Alina turned to face him. Leaning against the base units, she took a sip of wine and said, 'How's that?'

'You told PC Rigg to bag up her glass.'

'It seemed a good idea at the time.' She shrugged. 'I'm a medical professional and I have a weakness for cop shows.'

'It was a good idea,' he said, studying her closely. 'But there were only Kitty's fingerprints on the glass.'

'Isn't that a little odd? Surely the prints of the waiting staff should be on the glass too?'

'They were all wearing gloves. Mrs Blenkinsop's idea, apparently. She wanted them to look smart.'

'I see,' said Alina. 'But two things occur to me, Inspector. One, if I were putting poison into a glass, would I need to *touch* the glass and two, these days, surely everyone knows that you need to wear gloves?'

'How *did* you know it was poison?' Laidlaw retorted, placing his hands on his hips.

Alina broke out into a laugh.

'What's so funny?' he said.

Alina cleared her throat. 'Sorry,' she said. 'I suddenly had an image of you with a gun and a badge on your belt. I did say I have a weakness for cop shows. Most of them are American.'

DI Laidlaw's face paled. 'I had a gun in my last job,' he whispered. 'I never want to carry one ever again. Now, how did you know it was poison?'

Alina swallowed, knowing she'd crossed a line she had not been aware existed. 'Easy,' she said. 'You already told me it wasn't natural causes. I knew from her patient records that she was in good health. She clearly wasn't strangled, drowned or shot. So that means imbibing something, such as a form of poison.'

'I can see I'm going to have to keep my eye on you,' he said, taking the proffered mug of coffee. He looked at the coffee mug and back to Alina.

'Don't worry, Inspector, if I was planning on poisoning you, I wouldn't do it here in my own home.'

He sniffed at the coffee and took a tentative sip. 'How are your stocks of gloves, Nurse Merrycott? Any missing?'

'Inspector, I keep count of the boxes of gloves, not the individual items. And didn't you say all the waiting staff were wearing gloves? Surely there was ample opportunity to take a pair of gloves from the kitchen?'

'Perhaps,' he replied. 'That's not what I came to ask you though. Did you see anyone go near Mrs Blenkinsop while you were on the dance floor?'

Alina pursed her lips. She'd been focused on keeping Fitz's wandering hands at bay, but she saw no reason to tell DI Laidlaw that tidbit. 'I didn't see anyone put anything in her glass, if that's what you're asking. I saw her and Ralph have another little contretemps, then I saw one of the waitresses bring her a fresh glass of wine and take the empty one away.'

'I see,' he said, taking a sip of the hot coffee. 'You said she wasn't popular?'

'I did,' said Alina. 'But no one hated her enough to kill her.' She stopped, biting her lip. But perhaps there were… at the moment she could think of three people, four if she included herself.

'Reverend… Alina, if you know anything you must tell me. It could put you in danger if you don't tell me everything you find out.'

'Danger?' The thought surprised Alina. 'I thought I was a suspect?'

'Well, technically you are, but only technically. I don't think you're a killer. After all, you're a nurse and a vicar.' He smiled at her, flushing slightly as he finished the last of the coffee.

'Nurses have killed before,' replied Alina. She led the way to the front door, opened it and stood to one side.

DI Laidlaw stood on the step for a moment, as if he were about to say something else, but he suddenly gave her a sharp nod and strode away.

Alina watched him disappear and then reluctantly closed the door.

'He was gorgeous, Mum! Who was he?' Claire called from the top of the stairs. She ran down, taking the steps two at a time, and followed Alina into the kitchen. 'Is supper nearly ready? I'm starving.'

'Yes, of course,' Alina replied to the second question. 'Almost done. It's a Mrs Sullivan special.'

'Apples *and* sultanas?' Claire rolled her eyes.

'Yes, but it's very kind of her to help me out. She doesn't have to.'

'Okay,' said Claire, folding her arms. 'Well?'

'Well what?' Alina took the heated curry and rice dishes from the oven and placed them on the kitchen table. 'Cutlery, sweetheart,' she said.

Claire placed spoons and forks either side of the two place mats. 'Come on, Mum. Fess up. Who was he?'

'He's the policeman who might arrest me for murder if I can't find out who killed Kitty Blenkinsop.' Alina winked at her daughter but, all the same, she slumped onto the kitchen chair nearest the hob and fanned herself with a napkin.

'For real?' Claire dug her fork into the dish, speared a chunk of chicken and popped it in her mouth.

'Yes, for real.' Alina smiled at the phrases her teenage daughter came out with. 'Do you want some naan?'

'Please,' replied Claire. She took a hunk of the Indian bread and tore a large piece off, dunking it in her curry and placing it in her mouth. 'Wasn't—'

'Manners, Claire,' sighed Alina. 'Don't speak with your mouth full.'

Claire grinned, wiped her hands on her napkin and picked up her fork again. 'Wasn't Kitty Blenkinsop the one with a reputation for being nasty?'

'Let's just say she wasn't the most popular person in the village,' replied Alina.

Claire nodded her head sagely. 'So everyone hated her?'

'That's not what I said.'

'Oh, I know, you never say anything nasty, Mum, but I've learnt to read the subtexts.'

'You're only fourteen. What on earth can you know about subtexts in conversations?'

'You send me to a boarding school. It's a dog-eat-dog world,' Clare replied. She looked at her mother through lowered lashes.

Alina couldn't tell if she was joking or not. Perhaps she should have a quiet word with the headmistress?

Claire picked at the bread. 'Anyway, he could have told you everything he said over the phone. I reckon he likes you, that's why he called round.'

'He said he was just passing and saw the lights on.' Warmth spread across Alina's face, and it wasn't from the curry or the heat still emanating from the oven.

'Ha!' said Claire, pointing her fork at her mother. 'You like him too. I can see it. Has he asked you on a date yet?'

'Claire, darling, he's still working on a murder enquiry. He probably wanted to see my face when he said the murder weapon was poison,' said Alina. 'Now, please stop waving that fork around.'

Claire placed the fork beside her plate and bowed her head. 'Are you going to solve this one too?' she said.

'Solve what?' Alina choked on a mouthful of chicken and rice. It had never occurred to her that Claire knew.

'Like you solved Daddy's disappearance,' Claire replied. Her wide eyes pooled with tears. 'The police thought you'd killed him, but you proved you didn't. Are you going to do the same again?'

'Claire. Sweetheart. I didn't do anything. I just made the police realise that I'd stayed home with you. I still don't know what happened to your father.' Alina lowered her gaze and gripped her napkin in her lap, knuckles white against the pale blue cloth.

'I don't think he's dead,' said Claire.

Alina blinked teardrops onto the napkin, darkening the material. 'Not this again,' she sighed. 'Why on earth do you keep saying that?'

'I have my reasons,' replied Claire. She drew her lips into a tight line, and white-faced, ate the rest of her supper in silence.

Alina's mind raced. She'd waited longer than the required seven years to declare Jake dead. All due diligence had been carried out. Her father, a solicitor, had ensured everything had been done correctly. If Jake Merrycott was still alive, he didn't want to be found. He'd not taken a penny from their joint bank account after he left their home to buy milk. Not that night, nor any of the nights afterwards.

For weeks Alina had waited for him to return. During those weeks the police investigated her. Had she killed him? How? How did she get rid of his body? Finally, the telephone evidence that she'd been speaking to her mother while Jake wandered off into the night came through. She was exonerated, but even now—over twelve years later—she still wanted to know where he'd gone.

When Claire rose to rinse her plate and put it in the dishwasher, Alina jumped. Pulled out of her reverie, they exchanged glances but no one spoke.

Alina was grateful when she heard Claire's bed creak and the click of the light being switched off. Suddenly, feeling very alone, Alina put her head in her hands and sobbed.

CHAPTER SIXTEEN

'Poison, you say?' Fitz said the following morning, giving the mug of coffee a stern look before raising it to his lips. 'Do you know what sort?'

Claire had declared to her mother that Major Fitzgerald was an old bore, and retired to her bedroom after brunch to complete her homework. Judging by the volume of the music coming from her room, Claire's homework was either not being done, or she was researching the impact of loud music on teenage deafness.

'No idea, he didn't say. And the coffee's fine, Fitz,' said Alina, folding her arms. 'I'm not trying to poison you. No one is. Well, not as far as I know.'

'But poison is a woman's weapon,' replied the major.

'Nonsense,' said Alina. 'That's a very old-fashioned idea. There are lots of reasons why a person might use poison to kill someone.'

'Such as?' snorted the major.

'One, someone might be physically weak, someone who is old or infirm,' said Alina. She counted off on her fingers. 'Or they could be squeamish. Or they might simply want to be somewhere else when the death occurs. Perhaps allowing for a time lapse to create an alibi?'

'So not just a woman's weapon then?' said Fitz.

'No, and stop being sexist,' said Alina. 'In all the crime novels, they say you need to know everything about the victim to work out why someone would kill them. Why would anyone kill Kitty?'

'You did meet her, I take it?' offered the major.

'That's not very helpful.' Alina selected some goat's cheese from the platter in the middle of the kitchen table, and spread it over a cracker. 'Not everyone hated her.'

'I think a fair few did.'

Alina narrowed her eyes as she pushed the cracker in her mouth. 'Like who?'

'Well if last Saturday night is anything to go by, Ralph Pomeroy for one. And who did you say she was shouting at when you got to the golf club in the afternoon?'

'Joanne Stokes. But Jo wouldn't hurt a fly. She's a very gentle person,' said Alina.

'You've not heard her bawling at Frank when he's slow getting the fish ready and she's got a queue,' muttered the major. 'I wouldn't like to get on the wrong side of her.'

'That's not a side of her I've seen,' said Alina. 'She's always kind to me.'

'That's women for you,' said the major. 'Devious.' He stabbed the kitchen table with his forefinger as if to make the point.

'You're being sexist again,' said Alina. 'Who else would have it in for Kitty?'

'Did she argue with anyone else on Saturday?'

'I just saw the arguments at the golf club with Ralph—oh, and with Tracy Goring. I didn't see any others.'

'What about the argument over the flowers?' asked the major.

'That was on Friday.' Alina thought for moment. 'She was complaining about freesias being used instead of African violets. Amy Pretty and Fiona Pomeroy were there.'

'Well there you go, then,' the major said. 'That's two more suspects for you.'

'Over a few flowers? I can't believe it! I was astonished by the argument, but to kill over it makes no sense at all. Although…' Alina hesitated, her mind drifting back to the events of the previous Friday and Saturday. Had anyone been angry enough to kill Kitty?

'Would it have been just over the flowers?' said the major, scarcely seeming to notice her silence. 'Or, is it more likely that someone was fed up with how she treated everyone?'

'Yes,' said Alina. 'Perhaps. I went to the Women's Guild meeting on Tuesday evening. Fiona told me that Kitty was a blackmailer.'

'Really? That's interesting. Who was she blackmailing?'

'I'm not sure. Fiona hinted that it was over Ralph and Tracy and her last baby.'

Fitz nodded. 'It seems to me that Kitty was more likely to be a victim of blackmail, rather than the blackmailer.' He stroked his moustache. 'Who else did Kitty argue with?'

'She shouted at me, at Jo Stokes, at Amy Pretty and Fiona Pomeroy,' Alina replied. 'Then before the dance, she was shouting at Ralph Pomeroy. And that poor waitress could do nothing right.'

'Well that's a nice set of suspects for you,' said the major. He ran his eyes over the cheese board and selected the Blue Stilton, slicing though the creamy blue veins. 'Any front runners?'

'Amy,' said Alina. 'I went into the wool shop on Saturday. Because Kitty was persuading everyone to shop online or in the big craft shops in town, Amy's business was struggling, and she's dependent on that for her retirement fund.'

'Well, if that's true, my dear lady, loss of income and financial security are very good reasons to kill someone. Don't you think?' Fitz rose and placed his cap on his head.

'I suppose so, it's just... oh, I don't know. I can't imagine Amy hurting anyone,' sighed Alina, as she followed him to the front door. She ambled back to the kitchen, picked up the plates and rinsed them before placing them in the dishwasher.

Outside a blackbird dug in the gaps between the flagstones, dragging lumps of moss aside. Each lump was pecked and thoroughly inspected for insects. He looked up at Alina, tilting his head to one side, before he flew to safety on the fence, black eyes still trained on the moss. 'Blackmail?' Alina muttered to the bird. He cocked his head to the other side. 'Or money? The love of money?' The blackbird shook himself and flew off, leaving Alina to her thoughts. Kitty had loved money, but had someone else loved their own money enough to kill for it?

'You don't really think Tracy Goring would sleep with Ralph Pomeroy, do you?'

Alina started. She'd not heard Claire on the stairway. Too shocked to wonder how her fourteen-year-old daughter knew about sex, she stood slack-jawed by the Aga.

'He's too old, for one,' Claire snorted scornfully. 'She'd fancy someone much younger. Like that gardener who was there last summer. He'd be much more her type.' Claire sliced a portion of Brie, placed it on her plate with a handful of crackers and strolled back to her homework.

Alina thought about the young groundsman from the golf club. He'd definitely have been more attractive to a young woman than Ralph.

. . .

Leaving Claire with her homework, Alina decided to take a walk on the beach. She needed a ponder and it was her favourite place to think. Her heart slowed with the rhythm of the waves as she plodded along the shoreline, lost in her thoughts.

Poor Kitty, she'd upset everyone she'd ever met. Alina found herself wondering about the famous Reg Blenkinsop. Had that been a happy marriage? Kitty constantly sang praises for the life they had together. Had it been so wonderful? How would *she* talk about Jake if anyone asked?

Since it was still a little early in the season for too many tourists, the beach was quiet. Alina squealed when a small wave coasted around her foot. The cold water seeped over the edges of her shoes and onto her socks. *You should have put your boots on, silly.* Deciding to turn back in a few more steps, Alina kicked some stones over, the puzzle going around and around in her head. Fitz was right in some respects; poisoning was subversive. It didn't need strength or vigour, or even to be in the same room as the victim. Were any of her suspects so underhanded? No, Ralph would use his hands. Men do, she thought. And Amy? Tracy? Where would they even get hold of poison?

Alina shivered as if the sun had gone behind a cloud. She looked around and found herself surrounded by seaweed-covered posts; she had ambled out of the sunshine and under the pier.

The waves were fiercer here, crashing into the posts and sending pebbles flying into the air. Alina raised her jacket collar, pleased that she'd thought to grab it before leaving the house.

Movement spied from the corner of her eye made her twirl around. But the isolation under the pier was absolute. On the back of her neck, soft fine hairs arose and her skin prickled. She twisted her wedding ring. *Nonsense, you're becoming fanciful in your old age.* Time to go back to the cottage. She marched back into the sunshine, instantly feeling better with the warmth on her face, but out of fear of what she might see, Alina decided not to snatch a glimpse behind to ascertain if she'd really been alone.

Later, before bed, Alina called for Thalia, resting against the front door post while she waited for the cat to deign to return. She breathed in the night air. As she was about to give up and leave the imperious animal outside for the night, Thalia appeared from under the lavender bush, rubbing her head on Alina's ankles. She picked the cat up for a cuddle. Thalia yowled, wriggled, and jumped to the ground. She strolled into the house with her tail erect and her head held high. On the point of following her cat's lead, Alina pushed herself away from the door frame. Then she heard it. The unmistakable two-tone of an ambulance siren. The vehicle shot out of a side street and down the High Street heading out of town, the noise fading into the distance.

Alina waited until all was silent again, wondering who of her neighbours needed such urgent medical help. She went inside, bolting the door firmly behind her. A cup of herbal tea would settle her and help her sleep. In the kitchen she filled the kettle and prepared a mug and tea bag. Her phone buzzed and skimmed across the kitchen table. Glancing at the kitchen clock and frowning, she reached over, pressing her index finger against the lock.

Dr McCarthy.

I've just been with Amy Pretty. She's been poisoned. Hopefully got to her in time.

CHAPTER SEVENTEEN

Grateful for the thin cardigan under her cassock, Alina stood shivering outside the church as stubborn clouds filled the sky. Summer often came late to the exposed eastern coast. She waited to bid farewell to her parishioners. Everyone had learned about the ambulance last night, even those whose homes were too far away to have heard any noise from the sirens. All had noticed Amy Pretty's absence from the front pew. Sirens weren't often heard in Eastwold, and speculation was rife.

Alina's prayers for those too ill to attend today's service did nothing to reduce the rumours; it only increased the gossip, but she was anxious to give nothing away to the questioners as they left the church. As she bid goodbye to the stragglers, she noticed how the locals gathered at the kissing gate, still chattering away. She'd spoken to Dr McCarthy before the service and knew it was touch and go for the old lady. Amy's condition shouldn't be common knowledge just yet but, once again, lack of information made no difference to the chatter.

'I've been thinking about what you said yesterday, Alina.' Major Fitzgerald strolled on the footpath alongside her as they wandered to Lighthouse Cottage. He had somehow invited himself back for late elevenses after the morning service.

'You have?' replied Alina. 'What did I say exactly?' Her mind was still on Amy Pretty, and she'd missed the major's comment.

'You said that there is always a reason why someone is killed. You were quoting that little French chappie in the Agatha Christie novels.' Fitz waved his hand as if to shoo her interruption away.

'He was Belgian,' said Alina with a sigh, twisting her door handle and stepping into the cottage. She headed towards the kitchen and the kettle.

'Not the point,' said Fitz. 'It was something about "why them" and "why now". Who needed Kitty and Amy out of the way?'

'I can't imagine anyone would want Amy out of the way, apart from Kitty.' Alina scratched her head with the end of her pencil.

'And vice versa, don't you think? Didn't Amy tell you Kitty was destroying her business?'

'True,' said Alina.

'Write it down then,' said Fitz, stabbing the notepad with his forefinger. 'Write it down.'

'How come I'm writing and you're doing nothing?' complained Alina. 'I am trying to prepare lunch for my daughter as well.'

'I'm doing the thinking,' said Fitz.

He stuck his chin out and, rather uncharitably, Alina decided he looked remarkably like Toad of Toad Hall, but all the same she picked up the notepad and pencil.

'Come on,' he said. 'Who else would want Kitty dead?'

'The waitress from last Saturday?' mused Alina. 'She scowled at Kitty all evening.'

'Which one?'

'Tracy Goring. Skinny girl, three kids. Lives in Norton Road.'

'Oh her…' said Fitz. 'I think you can forget about her. She scowls at everyone.'

Alina pursed her lips, but all the same she wrote Tracy Goring on the notepad. 'Anyone else?' she asked.

'There's you,' grinned Fitz.

'Nonsense,' said Alina. 'Why would I kill her?'

'Jealousy over me, I'm told,' Fitz scooted his chair away from the kitchen table, holding up his hands as if to ward her off. 'It's only what I'm told, Alina. You don't want to share me.'

'Stuff and nonsense,' Alina retorted. 'Any other serious suggestions? What about Kitty's many liaisons with married men? Or is that just idle gossip?'

'I don't think it's without some truth,' mused Fitz. 'I think there's many a fair lady in this town who would be happy to see the back of Mrs Blenkinsop.'

'Any front runners?' asked Alina. 'Linda Crawford, perhaps?'

'Let me give it some thought,' replied Fitz. 'In the meantime, I have other news. I've done some digging into Mrs Blenkinsop's past.' He returned his chair to the table and sat back, laying his hands flat on the kitchen table and smiling expectantly.

'What have you found out?'

He huffed, clearly disappointed that he wasn't getting any praise. 'They knew each other in the old days.'

'Fitz, are you going to make me beat this out of you?'

Alina laughed. 'Who are *they?* Just tell me what you know and enough of the suspense.'

'Very well. Kitty Blenkinsop's husband, Reg, was a cereal manufacturer. A very successful one. Kitty was his second wife or perhaps the third.' He pulled a small black notebook from his breast pocket, shuffled through his notes and, unable to find the information he needed, looked up at her pleadingly.

Alina folded her arms. 'Carry on.'

'Reg had, for a number of years, a faithful secretary,' Fitz scratched his chin. 'I think they're called personal assistants these days. Anyway, there were rumours he was having rumpy-pumpy with his assistant.'

Alina sniggered as she walked to the oven to check on the roast. 'I don't think that's what it's called these days.'

Fitz frowned at the interruption. 'Yes, that's as it may be, but guess who that assistant was?'

'Amy Pretty?' Alina wafted herself with a tea towel before putting the beef back in the Aga. 'I'd invite you to stay to lunch, Fitz, but it's my last meal with Claire before she goes back to school.'

Fitz waved her explanation away. 'No matter,' he said. 'You're right about Amy though. How did you know?'

'Call it a wild guess. Did the affair continue when he married Kitty?'

'According to my source, it did. And Kitty wasn't at all happy. And especially not when she found out about the child.'

'Child?' Alina held onto the Aga before returning to the table and sliding onto a chair opposite Fitz. 'What happened to it?'

'Adopted, apparently. I'm still trying to find her, but so was Kitty.'

'Why would she want to find her husband's love child?' Alina frowned, pushing a curl behind her ear.

'That I don't know. But it can't be good, either for Amy or the child. My source thinks it was so Kitty could embarrass Amy and make her a laughingstock, what with Amy being so prim and proper and all that.'

'That would be an awful thing to do. So spiteful and unnecessary. Poor Kitty! She must have been in terrible pain.'

'You're more forgiving than I'd be, Vicar,' said Fitz. 'As for why, I know that too. It seems that Reg bought the shop for Amy, *and* her little cottage. But if the business fails, she loses her pension pot as you said.'

'But if she owns the building she'd still be able to sell it,' Alina said. 'Plus it still doesn't seem enough to kill over. And she'd get good money for the cottage. She could move away. Buy somewhere smaller and live off the proceeds.'

'You're right. I'm stumped,' said Fitz, putting his elbows on the table and sinking his chin into his cupped hands. 'I thought I had it solved for a moment.'

'Well it does give Amy more motive than we thought initially,' Alina said, smiling at him and cutting another slice of cake. 'Selling up and moving away would mean Amy would lose all her friends.'

The major brightened up as she slid the slice of Victoria sandwich onto his plate.

'But I still don't see how she could have got hold of poison.'

'Cricket club,' mumbled Fitz through a mouthful of cake.

'Pardon?'

'She was secretary for the cricket club for years. Gave it up when she turned seventy. Said it was a younger person's job. That lass in Norton Road you mentioned? Tracy Goring. She took the job on, but all she got out of it was Ethan.'

Alina clasped her hands together as if in prayer. 'What has the cricket club got to do with poison?'

'Oh, there's a couple of tubs of cyanide left in the groundskeeper's shed. It's not pure, but I think he got it from a friend of a friend, if you understand my meaning. There were several wasps' nests under the clubhouse. The old groundskeeper used it to get rid of them.'

Alina shuddered thinking of the painful but hopefully quick death of God's beautiful creatures. Not everyone's favourites, but you had to admire their smart yellow and black uniforms. 'How many other people know about the groundsman's shed?' she said.

'Probably the whole village. He had loads of work afterwards. He was destroying wasps all that summer and the next. I think he killed wasps in every village for miles around.'

'But that means anyone could have known about the poison. Is it kept under lock and key?'

'Er, it was,' said Fitz. He scratched the top of his head. 'But *if* I remember correctly, at the last meeting, Tracy reminded us that the lock had been broken for several months and needed replacing.'

Alina raised her eyebrows and waited.

'Oh,' he said. 'I see what you mean. Broken lock. Anyone could have had access to the cyanide.'

'Yes, Fitz. Exactly,' said Alina. 'And from what you've told me, the entire village knew it was kept there. This doesn't narrow things down. It blows the whole case wide open. Anyone could have got the poison, and anyone could have killed her. We need to let the inspector know.'

'He's not going to be very happy,' said Fitz. He eyed the cake and Alina gave him the last slice, knowing that Claire wasn't going to be at all happy.

'Is there anyone else who would have wanted to kill Kitty?' asked Alina.

'Well,' said Fitz, 'It's like I said to the inspector. The only people who'd have wanted to kill her were the ones who'd met her.'

Alina stared at him, horrified at what he'd said but, deep down, she knew it was true.

No one had liked Kitty Blenkinsop.

CHAPTER EIGHTEEN

Claire dumped her school bag and backpack in Delia's boot. Alina locked it and they both sat in the front of the car. Alina closed her eyes and stroked the steering wheel as she turned the key.

'You need to get a better car, Mum,' said Claire. 'Something more reliable.'

'I like this car,' replied Alina, flashing a grin at her daughter as the engine finally caught and rumbled into life. 'I have lots of happy memories with this car.'

'That's partly my point.' Claire chewed the edge of her thumb. 'Don't you think you're living in the past? I worry about you.'

'That's not your job,' Alina said, biting her bottom lip. 'I'm supposed to worry about you. Unsuitable boys, your grades, and so on.'

'That major's not suitable,' Claire retorted. 'He's too old.'

'He's been very kind to me,' Alina said. 'He was my first friend in the village. It's not easy moving somewhere new.'

'Well, duh!' said Claire. 'I'm the one who got dumped in a new school, remember?'

'I thought you were settling in? Making friends?'

'I am, but I had lots of friends at my old school. Now I still feel like I'm the new girl.'

'But it's been nearly a year, darling. Surely there have been other new girls since you?'

'There have, but… oh, I don't know. I guess I still miss my old friends.' Claire picked at a hangnail, thrusting her thumb in her mouth when she made it bleed.

Alina's heart squeezed. Claire looked like a baby again. Stop it, she told herself, you *do* need to move on. Now who's living in the past?

'I'm sorry you had to change schools, Claire, but you couldn't have stayed at the other one with no home to go to at night.' Alina gripped the steering wheel, her knuckles whitening. *This isn't fair.* She took a deep breath and released it slowly. 'This is a good school and you're close enough that we can have these weekends together. That's a good thing, surely?'

'I know,' said Claire. 'I'm sorry. I guess we're both struggling to put the past behind us.'

'It's been hard for both of us, darling,' Alina replied soothingly. 'I miss you so much, but I wouldn't be able to look after you during the week. Not with two jobs. I'm sorry.'

'Mum, I get it. I do understand. I just miss you.'

'And I miss you too, sweetheart.'

The rest of the short journey took place in silence. Meredith College *was* a good school, Alina told herself, and it was only a few miles away. She blinked back a tear, wishing that Claire could be with her every single day, but knowing it would mean Claire would spend far too much of her time alone, with only Thalia for company. It was spending excessive amounts of time alone that had led to the trouble Claire found in London.

Thinking back to the conversation about Jake, Alina

wondered why Claire was so sure he was still alive. *Has she heard from him?* Goosebumps rose on Alina's arms at the thought of him returning to their lives. If he was still alive, where had he been all this time? He'd always kept... unusual company. Deep down, she'd always suspected a criminal involvement. Her first assumption when he went missing was that he'd been murdered, but she had no proof, and no desire to dig into his past, scared of what she might find.

Alina drove up the driveway to the imposing front entrance. Normally girls were not allowed through this door, but, after a weekend out, they had to be checked back in by a senior member of staff.

Alina twisted in her seat, but Claire had already jumped out of the car. She opened her door and leapt out. 'Claire,' she said, 'I know now isn't the time, but we'll talk about your dad when you come home next time. I promise.'

'Yeah, sure. You say that, but—'

'I mean it,' Alina said. She held her arms open and Claire stepped into the hug. 'I don't want you to worry, that's all,' she whispered into her daughter's dark hair.

'I'm not worried,' said Claire. 'But, yes, we do need to talk about him. If you don't tell me, then I'll have to start digging into the past for myself. See you next month, Mum.' Claire gave her a peck on the cheek and sauntered away up the steps to the huge doors without a backward glance.

Alina watched Claire's back until the doors closed firmly behind her. She let out a deep breath, patted Delia's steering wheel, and drove away.

Letting herself in the front door of Lighthouse Cottage, she was greeted by Thalia, winding herself around Alina's legs.

'Have you been neglected, puddy-tat?' Alina scooped her up and collapsed onto the sofa. Thalia snuggled close under

Alina's chin, purring loudly while Alina rested her head against the cushions and thought about Claire's last remark. She trembled, worrying what Claire could dig up about her father. Despite knowing that her daughter could be eminently sensible, she'd still got involved with a shoplifting gang. At least the police caution had had the desired effect, and the change of school had separated her from those so-called friends. Alina bit her lip, remembering how headstrong she'd been at the same age and, of course, meeting Jake Merrycott.

Auburn hair scraped off her face, teenager Alina Wilson looked around the concourse of Paddington Station. People with heavy cases pushed past her and cursed, so she cowered by the wall until the train emptied and the throng had gone. Exhausted, she slid down the wall and sat on the cold floor, chewing the end of one curl that had come loose from her ponytail, until a train conductor shooed her out of the station.

Once in the street she gasped at the noise and acrid smell of a busy day in London. Pulling her rucksack further up her arm, she crossed the road and went into a café. A cup of tea and a bacon sandwich later, she felt better, but she still had nowhere to sleep, and knew no one. Had this been such a good idea after all? Hanging her head, she thought about her parents and her sister. Would they have even noticed she'd gone?

As she picked up the last crumbs of her sandwich on the end of her forefinger, a man slipped into the chair opposite. 'Still hungry?' he said.

Alina narrowed her eyes, trying to look grown up and in control, but her lower lip gave her away.

He grinned. 'Runaway?

She nodded, brushing tears off her cheek with one hand. His hazel brown eyes were soft and gentle. Despite everything she'd been told about strangers, she felt a connection with this man—as if he were someone she could trust.

'You're lucky I found you then,' he said. 'Not some pervert. My name's Jake. I hope you're not planning on sleeping rough tonight?'

Alina shook her head. 'No,' she mumbled.

'I've got a place. You'll be safe with me,' he said. 'That your bag?'

Alina nodded, and he hefted her rucksack onto one shoulder and held out his hand to her. Before she had time to think, she took his hand and followed him out of the café.

With her rucksack now on his right shoulder, Jake strolled down a side street and turned a corner into a narrow road. All the houses were boarded up. Surely this can't be where he lives, thought Alina.

Halfway down the street, Jake rapped on a graffitied door. Alina noticed the rhythm, suspecting it was a special knock. The chipboard creaked open, just a crack, but then wider to allow Jake to enter. He dragged Alina over the threshold.

The floor was covered with hessian rugs and sleeping bags. A haze hung in the room, like the aftermath of a bonfire, but with a sweet, sickly smell. Alina blinked, trying to clear her head. Don't faint now, she prayed.

Jake dropped her rucksack on a sleeping bag in the corner and told her to make herself comfortable. Tears stung her eyes, but she clenched her jaw, determined not to cry again. Sitting on the sleeping bag, hugging her rucksack, she stared around the room. A woman with dyed red hair lay on the other side of the room, puffing on a cigarette, her movements languid and lazy. As she blew out the smoke, it mixed into the haze in the room. Alina wondered what kind of tobacco it was. It didn't smell like her father's pipe.

Jake and the other man talked in the kitchen—Alina could hear their voices but not the words, although the tone was not comforting.

The voices increased in volume.

'She's got nowhere to go.' Jake's voice was loud. Angry.

'She can't stay here,' Jake's companion shouted. 'She's a kid. Underage. The old bill will be looking for her.'

'Just tonight then,' Jake replied.

Jake was frowning when he returned to the room, but he held a bowl and a couple of slices of bread. He placed the bowl in Alina's lap. 'Eat up,' he said.

Alina stared at the baked beans and the unbuttered bread. Picking up the spoon, she shoved beans into her mouth, taking a bite of the dry bread. Forcing herself to chew, spoon by spoon, bite by bite, she finished her meal.

Jake's friend stood in the doorway and glared at her. Alina rose to take the bowl into the kitchen, pushing past him to leave the room.

It only took one look at the filthy kitchen for her to realise she wanted to go home.

CHAPTER NINETEEN

'Nurse Merrycott!'

Alina whirled around, shading her eyes from the bright sun, but she saw no one. Continuing on her way, she heard another shout.

'Vicar, wait up.'

Alina looked behind her again. DI Laidlaw was striding up the High Street towards her.

'Didn't you hear me?' he puffed at her, bending over to rest his hands on his knees.

'You're better off standing up if you're trying to get your breath back,' she said. 'More chance for the air to get to your lungs, rather than squashing them.'

'Thanks,' he puffed. 'I'm a bit out of condition.'

I wouldn't say that, Alina thought to herself. Aloud, she said, 'What can I do for you, Inspector?'

'The toxicology report has come back from the lab. Kitty Blenkinsop was poisoned, as you clearly suspected. It was cyanide. In her glass, again, as you also predicted. Are you sure there's nothing more you want to tell me?'

Alina stared at him. A crinkle formed in the lines around

his eyes. A hint of a smile. 'Are you serious, Inspector?' she asked, trying hard not to be distracted by the sun glinting on the silver threads on his temples. 'As your investigations may have discovered, Mrs Blenkinsop was... she was a difficult lady to—'

'Like?' said DI Laidlaw. 'Yes, that's coming through loud and clear. She was also a—'

'Blackmailer?' said Alina.

'Yes,' he said. 'That is something we're looking into. Tell me, Vicar, who's investigating this case? You or me?' Looking down at her, the frown was back.

'People talk to me, Inspector. I'm the spiritual leader of this community. What they tell me is in confidence.'

'But not under the seal of the confessional?' DI Laidlaw tilted his head to one side. 'You're Church of England, not Roman Catholic, aren't you?'

'Correct, Inspector, but in both my roles as vicar and as a nurse, I am expected to keep confidences, and as I already told you, I'm not a gossip.'

'In fact, Vicar, what you told me was that you don't listen to gossip. But, it appears you've been breaking that rule. Can I ask why? I hope you're not investigating my case?' His frown deepened and he placed his hands on his hips.

Alina folded her arms. *How dare he?* He was right though, she had been listening to gossip. Encouraging it even, and what kind of a person did that make her? She kicked at the gravel on the path, thoughts racing through her head. 'Don't lay the law down to me, Inspector Laidlaw,' she said.

A grin flickered across his face. 'Don't interfere in murder, Vicar. It could be very dangerous for you.'

'Is that a threat?' Alina drew herself up to her full height. Raising her chin, she looked him in the eyes and scowled. 'I do know how to take care of myself.'

'I'm sure you do,' he replied. 'But let's just call this a

friendly warning. Poisoning is a nasty business. It's insidious. Give me a straightforward stabbing any day. At least it's more honest.'

'Honest? That's a strange term.'

'What I mean is, if you shoot someone or stab them, or even hit them over the head, you're there. You're facing up to them. Poison always seems so underhanded to me. Deceitful.'

'Ah, so *you* believe it's a woman's weapon too? Major Fitzgerald would agree with you. Now, if there are no further questions, Inspector, I have a full list of patients to see.' Alina nodded as politely as she could, and strode off down the street. Insufferable man, she thought. But now she knew what type of poison had been used, she couldn't wait to tell Fitz that he'd been right all along.

However, before she could talk with the major, Alina had one more patient added to her visit list by the GP surgery and, not for the first time, she glowered at the tablet. Snatching her mobile from her pocket, she snapped, 'Is this a joke, Seda?'

'Hello Alina,' replied the receptionist. 'It's fine. Mr Mahoney has promised Dr McCarthy that he'll behave.'

Alina grunted, opened Delia's door, and sat behind the wheel. *Technically,* bad *is a behaviour too.* Pulling out from their parking spot in the town square, Alina and Delia chugged slowly out of town towards Cedric's cottage.

At the cottage door, Alina took the front door key from the Master Lock, replacing it as soon as the front door was ajar. She rotated the numbers and, with a deep sigh, pushed the door open. She stepped over the threshold with her medical bag gripped tightly in her hand.

'Cedric, it's Nurse Merrycott,' she called. There was no answer, but she marched to the doorway of his sitting room.

Sat in his armchair, Cedric turned his head and gave her a winning smile. Or at least his lips parted in a rictus-like manner, displaying his yellow teeth.

Alina shivered. 'I'm here to change your dressing,' she said.

Cedric nodded and tried to raise his feet onto the tattered footstool that was in front of his chair. 'That's fine,' he said.

Placing a spare pair of gloves on the carpet once more, Alina placed her bag beside the footstool and bent to her task. She flinched when the walking stick clattered to the floor.

Cedric cackled. 'How are you today, nurse?'

Alina raised her head, narrowing her eyes. *What is he after?* 'I'm fine, thank you.'

'I hear you're investigating the old bat's murder?'

'I'm not. Well, not really.'

'What does that mean? Either you is or you ain't.'

'I'm not, Cedric, and I'm not one to gossip.' *There was a time when you didn't lie either.*

'Come on, tell me what you know. What have you found out so far?'

Alina continued unwrapping the dressing on his other foot. She bit her lip, wishing she was far away from this conversation.

'Have you spoken with the Goring girl?'

Alina shook her head.

'You should. Kitty Blenkinsop was trying to get her evicted.'

'What on earth for?' The question leapt unbidden from Alina's lips, and she rolled her eyes under closed lids.

'Spite! But she was making accusations about a house of ill-repute.'

Alina hid a smile at the old-fashioned term. 'That doesn't seem very fair. Tracy seems like a nice girl.'

'It in't fair. Who else is in the frame?'

Alina gave up. 'Fiona Pomeroy said Kitty was a blackmailer.'

Cedric pursed his lips. 'Have you talked to the Pomeroys?' he asked. 'There's something off about them—that Ralph, especially.'

'I see,' said Alina, bending her head to the task of dressing his feet. 'I'll make sure I talk to them. Amy Pretty had problems with Kitty too though.'

'How is Amy?' Cedric said.

'I think she's okay,' said Alina. 'I'm going to see her next.'

Cedric nodded and reached for his walking stick. Alina placed it next to his chair. 'Talk to Ralph Pomeroy,' he said. 'He's always a bit too pleased with himself, but I've heard rumours about him losing his sister.'

CHAPTER TWENTY

Alina looked at the charts by Amy Pretty's bed. The old lady was recovering well from her ingestion of cyanide, better than most people, but Alina was still suspicious. Had it been a genuine attempt at suicide or was it a calculated attempt to put the police off her tracks? Alina sat down by Amy's bed and reached out to squeeze the elderly woman's pale, liver-spotted hand.

As Alina sat back in the chair, Amy's eyelids fluttered. Her eyes opened and she peered around the room, seemingly unable to focus. Snatching her hand away, and using her elbows, she pushed herself into a sitting position. Once upright, she rubbed her hands over her face and peered at Alina. 'Well, this isn't quite how I expected heaven to look.'

Alina gave Amy her brisk professional smile. 'I'm glad to see you awake,' said Alina. 'How are you feeling?'

Amy raised her eyes to the ceiling, as if the answer to the question lay there. 'I'm fine,' she sniffed.

'That was a very silly thing to do, Amy.'

'I know.' Amy twisted her hands in her lap. The enlarged knuckles were red and looked sore.

Arthritis, thought Alina. 'We can talk about it, in confidence, if that's what you'd like?'

'I was scared,' Amy replied. 'Nothing more than that. Lord knows, I've had my troubles with Kitty Blenkinsop, and I'm not sorry she's dead, but I didn't kill her, although that Inspector Laidlaw thinks I did.'

'I'm sure he doesn't,' soothed Alina. 'He's questioned everybody. He said he even considered me as a suspect at one point.'

'You?' Amy crossed her arms in front of her chest. 'Why on earth would he suspect you?'

'I think he started off suspecting everybody, now he's eliminating us one by one. I don't think he can decide which one of us did it.'

'I hated her, you know,' muttered Amy. 'Always have. I moved here to get away from her, but once her husband Reg died, she tracked me down and followed me, simply to torment me.'

'But why? Why would she do that?'

Amy gave Alina a long hard stare. 'I wasn't always the woman you see here,' she said. 'I was young once. I was pretty. Some even said I was beautiful.' Amy looked around. 'Have you got a tissue?'

Alina bent down and sifted through the contents of her small handbag. She pulled out a small plastic sachet of paper tissues and slid them across the bed covers. 'I'm happy to listen if you want to tell me,' she said.

Amy went back to twisting her hands, this time shredding the tissue with her fingers. She sighed deeply and began to relate the history she had with Mrs Blenkinsop.

Alina relaxed as best she could in a plastic hospital chair, amused to discover that Major Fitzgerald had been correct about most of the salient points. Including the child.

'Did she want money?' asked Alina.

'No, she appeared to have plenty of money. Surprising really, considering how much she always demanded out of Reg. She just seemed to want to make my life a misery. Especially when she found out about my baby.' Amy sniffed, took the shredded strips of tissue, rolled them into a ball, wiped her nose, and stuffed the ball of wet tissue under her pillow.

It took every ounce of Alina's self-control to stop herself from visibly shuddering. 'Where's the child now?' said Alina.

Amy shook her head. 'I have no idea. I'd love to know where my little girl is. Kitty always wanted a child. That's why she was so spiteful when she found out about Evelyn.'

'Evelyn? That's a lovely name,' said Alina.

'It's the name I gave her,' sighed Amy. 'But she was adopted, so it's unlikely to be the name she has now.' Tears rolled down her pink cheeks, and Alina took a tissue from the pack sitting on the old lady's lap and wiped her tears.

'I'm so sorry,' she said. 'I'm so very, very sorry.'

Again, Amy shook her head. 'It's not your fault, Vicar. It was just Kitty and her insane jealousy.'

'Can't you tell the inspector this?'

'I've tried. Lord knows I've tried. But he refuses to believe me. There were *lots* of other people who hated Kitty.'

Tilting her head to the side, Alina gave Amy a soft smile. 'Really? Can you tell me?' she said. Pulling at her ear lobe, Alina tried to ignore her inner voice—*you* are *encouraging people to gossip.*

'She had affairs with Fiona and Linda's husbands and then treated the wives like dirt. Linda especially hated her. Didn't you notice?'

'I sensed the tension between Fiona and Kitty, but I'm not sure I saw Linda anywhere near her.'

'That's how bad it was between them. Linda couldn't stand to be in the same room as Kitty.'

The curtains around the bed swished aside. 'That's enough now,' said the nurse. 'Miss Pretty needs her rest.'

Biting her lip at the untimely interruption, Alina nodded and kissed Amy gently on her icy cheek. 'I'll talk to the inspector again,' she said.

Alina drove carefully to the police station, well aware that she was inclined to drive too fast when annoyed. She was still angry when she pulled into the car park at the local station where DI Richard Laidlaw had set up his investigation headquarters. Jumping out of the car, she slammed the door behind her, too furious to think of the consequences for poor Delia. She marched down the corridor to the office she knew Richard Laidlaw was using and knocked once, sharply, striding in without waiting for an answer.

'Back so soon, Reverend? What can I do for you now?' If Richard Laidlaw was at all surprised at the manner of her entrance, he kept it well hidden. 'You seem determined to insinuate yourself into my case?'

'Amy Pretty!' Too angry to sit down, Alina paced the short distance in front of Richard's desk. She turned and, putting her hands on her hips, said, 'How on earth can you suspect her of murder?'

'As I recall, Reverend,' said Richard, pulling his office chair closer to the desk. 'I told you I had a number of suspects. You included. The fact that Miss Pretty has chosen to attempt suicide only makes me all the more suspicious.'

'You think she tried to kill herself? You haven't considered that somebody might have wanted to poison her?'

'Naturally, I've given that some thought, but Mrs Blenkinsop was given a large dose of cyanide, enough to kill a silver-back gorilla, and Amy Pretty simply took enough to make her sick. She was still able to call for help and get to hospital in time. In my line of work,' said Richard, 'that's something we find suspicious. It was all too convenient.'

Alina slumped in the chair opposite him. 'She could have died. And you would have been responsible.'

'I disagree,' DI Laidlaw replied. 'I am not responsible for her actions any more than I am responsible for yours.'

Alina scowled. 'I can't imagine Amy killing anyone, even though I know she has a very good reason.'

'Yes,' said Inspector Laidlaw. 'She has motive, and although no one can place her near Mrs Blenkinsop's glass, you could also argue she had the opportunity. But what about means? How did she get hold of the cyanide?'

'I really couldn't say, Inspector,' said Alina, wondering if the shed padlock had been replaced. Perhaps she should go and have a look for herself? She noticed the large bags under his eyes and wondered how much sleep he was managing to get.

'What about you?' Inspector Laidlaw steepled his fingertips and, resting his chin on his index fingers, stared at her. 'Do you have access to cyanide?'

'Not through my work, Inspector,' Alina said. 'But—'

'But you know something, don't you? Come on, tell me. I hate being lied to!' The inspector slammed his hands on the desk.

Alina started, shocked at his outburst of temper. She had to tell him. 'It's come to my attention that most people in the village knew where there was cyanide.'

'What the blazes do you mean?' DI Laidlaw leapt to his feet. 'Where?'

'At the golf club,' she said, after a long pause. 'There's a groundskeeper's shed. 'Apparently it's in there.'

'See, I told you never to look for the best in people. They always let you down.' He snatched up his desk phone and barked orders at the officer who had the misfortune to answer the call.

'I'm so glad I'm not in your line of work, Inspector Laidlaw,' replied Alina. 'I *always* get to see the best in people.'

He laughed. 'Even when they're hitting you with a walking stick?'

It was unexpected to hear him laugh. His whole face changed, becoming softer and more youthful. 'How did you hear about that?' she said. Raising her hand to her cheek, she tried to cover the hot flush rushing across her face.

'Oh, I have my sources. At least you resisted hitting him back.'

'It was a close-run thing, I can assure you.' Alina returned his smile. 'Why did you really want to talk to me?'

'Be careful of Amy Pretty,' he said. 'As far as I'm concerned, she's still a suspect. And I'm wondering if I should put you *back* on my list.'

'Me?' said Alina. 'I thought you'd discounted me?'

'You still have access to poisons and she was after your major.'

'He's not my major,' replied Alina. 'And in any case, Kitty Blenkinsop had her eye on a lot of men, if you listen to the gossip, which you assured me you do.'

'Touché,' said the inspector. 'But you assured me you *didn't* listen to the gossip either.' He cocked his head to one side and winked.

It was so quick that Alina wasn't sure if she'd imagined it. 'Well if that's all, Inspector, I'd better be going.' Alina rose, pushing the chair back and picking up her medical bag.

'No, not quite,' he said. 'There was at least one man she'd shown no interest in at all. Despite his very clear enthusiasm.'

Alina frowned. 'Really? Amy Pretty thought Mrs Blenkinsop had had an affair with every man in the village.'

He smiled, rising from his chair and strolling to his office door. He opened it. 'Ralph Pomeroy,' he said. 'Now isn't that interesting?'

'Is it? Ralph Pomeroy seems to be a very busy man. It's a wonder he maintains his golf handicap. I wouldn't believe everything you hear, Inspector.' Alina let herself out into the corridor. As the door closed, she was convinced she could hear him laughing. Amy was also convinced that Ralph and Kitty had been involved. Had Amy been wrong or was DI Laidlaw mistaken? Alina scratched her head, wondering who was misleading her.

CHAPTER TWENTY-ONE

Alina stood in the corridor outside DI Laidlaw's office, allowing his words to sink in. She pulled at her earlobe and frowned. Kitty Blenkinsop and Ralph Pomeroy? She hadn't put the two together, and now she wondered if she'd been blind to the game they were playing. Or had it been a game? Had their arguments been an elaborate plot to cover up an affair? But what was it Richard had said—that Kitty had shown no interest in Ralph? Certainly, she'd taken every opportunity to humiliate the man, but was that part of their plan to divert attention away from their affair?

Alina jumped when she heard a click from the door handle behind her. Clutching her handbag tightly, she sped down the corridor towards the lift. Head bowed, she peeked in the direction of Richard's office, and saw him strolling along the shiny corridor, coming to a halt in front of the coffee vending machine. She watched him prodding his pocket for change and selecting the correct coins. What more did he know that he wasn't telling her?

A ping from the lift brought Alina's attention back to the

present. She stepped in, and pressed the button for the ground floor, determined to find out more about Ralph Pomeroy and his secret liaisons. Unable to speak with Kitty, Alina opted for the next best thing —she'd talk to Fitz. Once reunited with Delia, she telephoned Fitz to say she was headed for home and suggested he meet her there.

'How was Miss Pretty?' Fitz had taken up what was fast becoming his usual seat at Alina's kitchen table.

'As well as can be expected,' Alina replied. 'The inspector thinks she did it on purpose to avoid being a suspect.'

Fitz dropped his head, tracing his fingertip along the patterns of the tablecloth. 'That's dreadful,' he said finally.

'That's not the worst part.' Alina thumped the teapot on the table and began pouring the dark liquid into mugs.

Fitz looked up sharply. He gave Alina a faint smile, then poured milk and spooned sugar into his mug. 'Agreed,' he said slowly. 'The worst part is, not only did she take cyanide, but she actually had some in her possession to take. Cyanide she could have used to kill Kitty.' He sipped tea and shook his head in disbelief.

Alina slumped into a chair. 'I know,' she said. 'But I can't believe it. She was so scared that the inspector would arrest her, she tried to kill herself. I've spoken to him, but he just says it makes her look more guilty.'

'Which of course it does. Who else could have wanted Kitty dead?'

'The inspector told me that Ralph had made a play for Kitty several times and she'd turned him down. DI Laidlaw thinks this is what caused the antagonism between them.'

'If it is true, it does explain why Ralph was angry with her, but is it enough to kill over? It's not as if it was public knowledge?'

'Not as far as I know. That particular rumour has never reached my ears. Could it be that Kitty was blackmailing Ralph? Threatening to tell everyone? To tell Fiona if he didn't pay her?'

'That seems more reasonable than blackmailing Amy Pretty, especially if the old lady's business is failing because of Mrs Blenkinsop.' Fitz gazed longingly at the plate of biscuits, just out of reach.

'I agree,' said Alina, sliding the biscuits towards him. 'How can we find out? It's not as if we can investigate her bank accounts and see if there were any large deposits.'

Fitz tapped the side of his nose. 'There are ways,' he replied.

Alina gave him a sideways glance. *What is his secret?*

'Blackmail still doesn't feel right,' she said. 'Amy describes Kitty as being insanely jealous about the baby. But blackmailing someone feels rather cold and calculated. I'm not sure the two emotions fit together. Arc you?'

'I don't know.' Fitz shrugged. 'I'm not really one for emotions.'

Alina gave him a sharp glance. 'When I spoke to Amy, she said that Kitty always seemed to have plenty of money. Apparently when Reg was alive she always pestered him for more. And then…' Alina paused as a conversation came back into her head. Wide-eyed, she stared at Fitz. 'Husband stealer,' she said.

'Pardon?'

'That's what Linda Cranford called her before the dinner-dance. "A husband-stealing witch". I thought it was odd at the time. Where is Linda's husband? I don't think I've seen him for a while?'

'Well he's not under the patio if that's what you're thinking,' Fitz sniggered. 'Nick moved to Woodbridge when Linda threw him out.'

'Was she relieved to be rid of him or did she blame Kitty?'

'I'm not sure.' Fitz took a gulp of tea, emptying the mug. He smoothed his moustache and pursed his lips. 'Linda doesn't look like her old self. She was always a smartly turned out woman. I don't mean the plastered in makeup type. She was classier than that, but now—'

'She doesn't seem to care how she looks.' Alina refilled Fitz's mug. 'She's been very strange with me since it all happened.'

'Strange?'

'Glaring at me. Not speaking. She's not stopped for a word after a church service in weeks. And now—' Alina drew in a deep breath, then let it go. 'She told Cedric Mahoney that I'm a suspect.'

Fitz snorted.

'It's not funny,' Alina retorted. 'Richard told me he considered everyone as a suspect until he'd eliminated them. That doesn't mean I'm any more under suspicion than Linda is.'

If Fitz had noticed her use of the inspector's first name, he said nothing.

'There's something else,' said Alina. 'Before the dinner-dance, Linda said she was surprised no one had swung for Kitty by now. Then Amy told me that Linda couldn't stand to be in the same room as Kitty. If that's true, why did Linda volunteer to help? Was she trying to get close enough to kill her?' Alina sighed. 'And now she's trying to get everyone to point the finger at me. I think that's really suspicious, don't you?'

'I don't know,' Fitz replied, studying his tea intently. 'She has the same motive and means as everyone else. However, no one saw her go near Kitty all evening until she was dead.'

'Someone in the crowd said, "good riddance" when Geoff declared Kitty was dead,' Alina said. 'I never saw who it was though, but I thought I saw Tracy Goring smile. Then, in the toilets, Linda was telling Amy she must be pleased Kitty was dead.'

'That's not nice behaviour,' Fitz said. 'But it doesn't make her a killer.'

'No, you're right, I suppose. Could you see what you can find out about this blackmailing business?'

Fitz nodded.

'Good,' said Alina. 'In the meantime, I'll have a chat with the other suspect on our list.'

CHAPTER TWENTY-TWO

When Alina visited Ethan Goring at the General Hospital the following day, she discovered he was recovering well, and was no longer in intensive care. Alina made her way to the children's ward, and after a short conversation with the ward supervisor she strolled to the far corner where Ethan was lying in bed, almost as pale as the white sheets covering him.

'Tracy?' she said. 'How are you doing?'

Tracy pushed herself into a sitting position and stared at Alina. Her face bore the creases of the bedsheets she'd rested on. 'Hello Vicar,' she said. 'I can't thank you enough for getting my Ethan into hospital.' She rubbed her hand over her face.

'You look exhausted,' said Alina. 'Why don't you come and have a cup of tea and something to eat in the café with me?'

'I don't want to leave him,' said Tracy.

'He'll be fine with us.' The ward supervisor had followed Alina to Ethan's bed. 'Go on, go and take a break. You've hardly rested in the last few days.'

Tracy stood. She was unsteady on her feet, as if her legs had not taken her weight for many days.

Alina offered the younger woman her arm and Tracy took it gratefully.

In the café, Alina sat Tracy down at a table and brought over cups of tea and a plate of sandwiches.

'Here,' she said. 'Eat these. You'll feel much stronger.'

Tracy opened three small packets of sugar, poured them all into her tea and stirred. 'Thank you,' she whispered. 'The paramedic told me you called them just in time. You probably saved his life.'

Alina shrugged. 'Just doing my job.'

Tracy nibbled on the edge of one sandwich. As she ate, colour began to return to her cheeks. There was silence while she finished the food and drank her tea.

'I'm not religious nor nothing,' said Tracy. 'I don't believe in your God.'

'I'm not here for that,' said Alina. 'I'm here to see how Ethan is and how you're bearing up. You do look *very* tired.'

'I'm shattered. I've got me mum up on the fourth floor, Ethan here and then I've still got two other kids who need looking after.'

'Who's looking after the other two while you're here?'

'Me sister's got 'em. She'll bring them back when Ethan's home again.'

'And your mother? How's she?'

'She's doing okay considering,' said Tracy. 'She had a stroke after a run-in with that old cow.'

Alina cocked her head to one side. 'Old cow?'

'Kitty bloody Blenkinsop! That's who.' Tracy pushed the plate and teacup away, ignoring the rattling of the crockery.

Alina picked up the teacup and stacked it on top of the plate, and moved the items to the far side of the table, out of

Tracy's reach. 'I didn't know about that,' said Alina. 'What kind of a run-in?'

'I don't really know,' sighed Tracy. 'It was down at the Women's Guild. I don't really know much more than that. It's not somewhere I go. It's not for the likes of me.'

'I thought the Women's Guild was for everyone?' Alina said cautiously. 'Isn't that the idea? Hence women's rather than ladies'.'

'Mum likes it. But they look down their noses at me,' said Tracy. 'It was all right before Dave left, but now I'm a single mum with three kids, they act as if I ain't good enough.'

'I'm sure that's not the case,' said Alina. She looked down at her hands, twisting her wedding ring and remembering Connie Wheeler's words. What a contrast Tracy's life was to her own time as a single mother.

'You ain't heard the gossip about me then?' Tracy looked at Alina through lowered lashes.

'I don't listen to gossip,' said Alina, unable to return the gaze.

Tracy sniggered. 'You should. Especially about me. I've got three kids all by different fathers—if you listen to the gossip, that is.'

'And is there any truth in that?' asked Alina.

'My eldest two are Dave's kids. Ethan... well that *is* a different story.'

Alina raised her eyebrows.

'Well, if you did listen to gossip,' Tracy said, 'you'd have heard that Ralph Pomeroy is Ethan's father.'

'But he's not, is he?' said Alina.

Tracy shook her head. 'No, he's not. But you can't tell the gossips that. They saw us laughing together at the shop and then I got pregnant, and so it had to be his.'

'Which shop?' Alina frowned. 'Fiona's?'

'Yes, Flowers by Fifi,' Tracy said. 'I've been working there on and off since I was fifteen. Fiona's great, or she was until that cow Kitty Blenkinsop stuck her big nose in.'

'Did Fiona believe the rumours?' Alina removed a clean tissue from a packet secreted in her handbag. She slid it across the table towards Tracy.

'No. No, not her. Like I say, she's always been kind to me. Mr Pomeroy always fancied himself, but he knew where to draw the line. Fiona is the one with the money. Not him. And anyway, he's a pompous old windbag. What on earth would I want with him?'

Alina pursed her lips. Claire had been right. There was no May and December love match here. 'Why did Dave leave?' asked Alina.

'He had the snip after the first two. So when I got pregnant again he knew it wasn't his.' Tracy leaned back in her chair and stared at the ceiling. 'Blighter hadn't told me he'd had the snip though. So when I told him I was expecting, he flipped. He just packed his bags and went. Not heard from him, and not had a penny from him since. Child support are chasing him.'

'And Ethan's father? Does he help out?'

Tracy sniggered. 'Nah, no such luck. He just wanted a quick fumble behind the clubhouse. He did a runner as soon as I told him.'

Alina clasped her hands together. At least she'd only been abandoned with one child and, she had all her family to support her. 'I'm sorry,' she said. 'You've not had much luck, have you?'

'No, you're right about that. I think Mrs Blenkinsop started the rumours about me and Ralph.'

'Why would she do that?'

'She was all about making people feel small,' Tracy pursed her lips, biting them into a thin line. 'Ralph Pomeroy tried his luck with her, you know.'

'You're not the first person to tell me that,' said Alina. 'When was this?'

'Not long before the rumours started.'

'How do you know?'

'I overheard them. Ralph was flirting with her when she came in the shop. I was out back dealing with a delivery order. She ripped him to shreds, said she wouldn't lower herself to sleep with him. He was furious. Called her all the names under the sun. She just laughed at him.'

'What happened then?'

'Nothing. She left the shop and not long after, the rumours started. That might even have been what her and Mum argued about,' Tracy sighed. 'Mum always helped out so I could earn a few quid here and there. Since her stroke, I've been on me own. I've got Kitty Blenkinsop to thank for that. I'm glad she's dead.'

Tracy stood, shoving her hands into the pockets of her skinny jeans. 'I better get back. Ethan will be wondering where I've got to. Thanks for the tea.'

Alina looked up and smiled. 'Thanks for the chat.'

Twisting in her chair, she watched Tracy walk away. The girl's stooped shoulders showed the weight of worry pressing down upon her. Was it enough to kill over? Alina wasn't sure. What she did know was that Tracy not only had the motive and the opportunity, but according to Fitz's information, she also had the means.

But, then again, so did Ralph Pomeroy.

CHAPTER TWENTY-THREE

On returning to Lighthouse Cottage, Alina found Mrs Sullivan on her knees on the kitchen floor with a dustpan and brush.

'What on earth's happened here, Mrs S?'

'That silly cat,' snorted Mrs Sullivan. 'Someone dropped off a nice cake for you. I put it on a plate, ready for when you came in and that… cat… knocked it on the floor.'

'Oh Thalia, what have you been up to?'

Thalia put her paws on the back of the kitchen chair, head tilted to one side, readying herself to be petted. Alina tickled the dark brown ears. 'Leave it, Mrs S. I'll finish cleaning up.'

Mrs Sullivan pushed herself to her feet. 'Well, if you're sure, Vicar. I like to get away on time.' She squeezed past Alina and collected her bag from the cloak stand. 'I've put your post on the side here, and that Fiona Pomeroy rang. She's left a message on the machine. You're invited to tea.'

'Thanks,' said Alina. In the peace which followed Mrs Sullivan's departure she finished cleaning the floor, sad to see the cake wasted. She decided to pop it on the bird table, then she fed the ravenous Thalia, and finally pressed the button on the answer machine. The hallway filled with the dulcet tones of Fiona Pomeroy.

'Oh, Vicar. I got your message. I rather think it would be better if you were to come to tea here at The Larches, don't you?'

Alina grinned. She needed to talk to Fiona and had invited her to Lighthouse Cottage, but she'd not seen inside the Pomeroy house. Joanne Stokes said it was spectacular, but Alina wondered what other secrets The Larches held. She raised her eyes heavenward and nodded. 'Thanks,' she said.

She picked up the handset and dialled Fitz's number. 'I've been invited to tea at Fiona Pomeroy's,' she said. She nodded whilst listening to the major's reply. 'Exactly. That's why I want you with me. I'll call her and find out when and let you know. Thanks Fitz.'

The Pomeroy's house was a large mock Tudor building. It fronted the Eastwold village green. A low box hedge prevented canine trespassers from using the lawn as a public facility. Alina wondered how successful it was. The iron railings at Lighthouse Cottage were a frequent stopping-off point for the local dogs. Behind the hedge were several large shrubs, all trimmed to within an inch of their lives. There was none of the cheerful chaos of Alina's little cottage garden, where wildflowers competed for space amongst the more traditional plants.

Fitz pulled into the driveway and turned off the engine. He removed his flat cap and smoothed his hair. 'Ready,' he said.

Alina gave him a tight-lipped smile, opened the car door,

and once she'd hauled herself out of the low-slung vehicle, brushed her skirt down.

Fitz nodded his approval. 'Mufti again, Vicar?' said Fitz. 'Probably just as well.'

Alina raised her eyebrows at him, frowning slightly before turning away and strolling to the front door.

Fiona Pomeroy must have heard the car because the door opened before Alina had a chance to knock.

Fiona was all smiles. 'Come in. I know it's a bit cool, but I thought we'd have tea in the orangery,' she said.

'Sounds splendid,' said Fitz, beaming.

They followed Fiona through the enormous house, into the kitchen, and to a large glass and steel edifice at the rear.

Alina looked at Fitz, her jaw dropping. He gave a grin. 'Quite something isn't it?' he said.

'I wasn't expecting something as grand as this,' admitted Alina.

'Ralph was an architect before he retired,' said Fiona. 'He does the odd design now and then, but mostly he plays golf.'

At the sound of his name, Ralph folded his newspaper and dropped it onto the floor under the table. 'Good afternoon both,' he said, standing up. 'Good of you to come.'

Ralph and Fitz shook hands, but to Alina's surprise, Ralph raised her hand to his lips and kissed it.

Alina tried her hardest not to snatch her hand back. She gave him a weak smile before sitting at the elaborate Victorian cast-iron table set. 'This is lovely,' she said. 'Thank you so much for inviting us.'

'Well, if you recall, we only invited you, Vicar,' said Fiona, primly. 'But we have come to understand that the two of you are quite inseparable these days.'

Alina's face warmed as she glanced at Fitz. She was rewarded with a large grin and a cheeky wink.

'Looks like our secret is out, Vicar,' said Fitz. He pulled

out one of the painted cast-iron chairs and sat himself down, reaching for a plate and loading it with sandwiches.

Alina was mortified; she didn't know where to look, but smiled at her hostess when Fiona handed her a tea plate.

'Please dig in, Vicar,' said Fiona. 'As you can see, there's plenty.'

The spread was delicious. Alina helped herself to two squares of salmon and cucumber sandwiches. She sipped at the tea Fiona had poured for her, gazing around the garden. 'You have a lovely garden,' she said. 'Have you always like flowers?'

'Yes,' said Fiona. 'Ever since I was a girl.'

Conversation was rather stilted. Any opening gambit was quickly shut down by Fiona Pomeroy, and Alina wondered how she could get their hostess to open up.

Attracted by the sugary treats on the cake stand, a wasp buzzed into the orangery. It hovered, and finally perched on a Bakewell slice. Ralph waved the newspaper at it, and the insect retreated, only to return seconds later.

'I thought you'd got rid of those things!' said Ralph to Fiona.

'I did,' she hissed. 'There must be another nest.'

'Best you find it soon,' sneered Ralph.

Alina coughed, politely. 'Perhaps you'd be so kind as to show me around the garden?'

Fiona flashed a grateful smile. 'I'd love to,' she said. 'Ralph?'

'I'll just stay here, with the newspaper, if you don't mind,' he replied. 'I'm a bit stuffed after all that food.'

'Me too,' said Fitz.

Leaving the men behind, Fiona led the way into the garden. She slipped her hand around Alina's arm and guided her past the borders filled with greenery. 'It's not quite at its best at the moment,' she said. 'I want everything ready for the yellow book day in the summer.'

'Yellow book?'

'It's an open garden event. We'll list our gardens in the yellow book, and people come and visit. It's another way of raising money locally. It's organised by the Women's Guild,' said Fiona.

Alina nodded. This was something else she needed to understand about this little town; her new home.

At the end of the garden the two women stopped, and Alina noticed an incongruous, bare patch of grass.

'It's the apple tree,' said Fiona. 'It sucks all the moisture out of the soil. It's on its way out but I can't bear to let it go.'

Alina looked up into the bare branches. 'Is it still alive?'

'Barely,' said Fiona. 'The wasps are sucking the last ounce of life out of it.'

Alina's gaze followed where Fiona pointed and, in the branches, she saw the conical shape of a wasps' nest. On the ground below the tree, several yellow and black striped bodies lay on the bare soil.

'I always think their nests are so beautiful,' said Alina.

'I hate them!' said Fiona. 'Nasty buzzy things. I don't see the point of them.'

'What happened to these ones?' asked Alina, prodding the bodies with the tip of her shoe.

'Poison,' said Fiona. 'Ralph got me some cyanide from the golf club.'

'I see.' Alina folded her arms and shivered.

'Are you getting cold, Vicar? Shall we go back in?' Fiona waved her hand in the general direction of the orangery, and the two women strolled back towards the warmth offered by the glass and steel edifice.

Stepping over the threshold ahead of her hostess, Alina

raised her eyebrows as Fitz and Ralph Pomeroy sprung apart.

'I was just showing old Fitz here how I keep my button-holes straight,' blustered Ralph. His face flushed and he stared over his wife's right shoulder as he waffled his explanation to her.

Alina watched them both. Fiona dipped her head, her face blank apart from the twitch underneath her left eye. Ralph folded over the lapel of his jacket to show them all the pin he used to secure his flower to his clothing.

Fitz glanced at Alina and nodded towards the house. 'Fiona,' she said, 'might I be permitted to use your facilities?'

'Of course,' replied Fiona. 'Go through the kitchen into the hallway. It's the last door near the front door.'

Alina made her way towards the toilet, but at the foot of the stairs she glimpsed framed black and white photographs hanging on the upper landing. Overcome by curiosity, she placed one foot on the bottom tread, waiting for it to creak. It didn't, and she trod on the next stair. Holding her breath and expecting to be discovered at any moment, Alina tiptoed up to the landing. In front of her was a series of photographs of two children. No, one was a little girl, the other an older sibling. Was that Fiona? Alina peered closer, wishing she'd brought her mobile phone with her to take a snap of the snaps. Yes, it was definitely Fiona with her arm around her little sister. The likeness was unmistakable, but Alina had always been under the impression that Fiona was an only child.

Hearing movement in the kitchen, Alina peered over the banister. It was only Ralph, getting ice, judging by the clattering sounds. She crept downstairs and into the cloakroom, flushing the toilet and washing her hands.

. . .

Fitz and Alina said their goodbyes and departed with waves and kisses and promises to meet again soon—it had been such fun after all.

'What do you suppose that was all about?' said Fitz, as he reversed off the driveway.

'I'm not sure,' said Alina. 'I had the feeling I was in some sort of Victorian farce. She invited me for a reason. Perhaps it would have been better if I hadn't taken you?' Alina pulled a face at Fitz. 'What on earth was all that about buttonholes?'

'I was asking Ralph about his relationship with Kitty when you and Fiona returned. I suppose he panicked,' Fitz replied. 'Did you find anything interesting when you went for your wander?'

'I did, as a matter of fact.' Alina adjusted her handbag on her lap. 'Photographs of Fiona as a child with a younger girl.'

'Cousin?' said Fitz.

'No, no they looked far too alike for that,' said Alina. 'They looked more like sisters. But, as far as *we* know, Fiona Pomeroy is an only child. I was told *Ralph* was the one who'd lost a sister. Any chance you could do some digging?'

Fitz nodded. 'Of course.'

'One day you're going to have to tell me how you get all your information,' said Alina. 'I almost suspect that you have contacts with the Secret Service.'

'Ah, now that would be telling.' Fitz smiled broadly and tapped the side of his nose with a gloved hand.

She turned to face him, but his expression, apart from a slightly raised eyebrow, gave nothing away.

CHAPTER TWENTY-FOUR

'Drink?' Alina called over her shoulder as she made the way to her kitchen, after Fitz had driven her home.

Fitz leaned against the kitchen doorframe, a slight smile on his lips. He smoothed his moustache. 'Yes, please. I could do with one after that... whatever it was!'

Alina took a half-full bottle of gin from the kitchen cupboard and received a thumbs up from the major. As she poured the drinks, she noticed the cake from earlier, still lying as she'd left it on the bird table. Scraps were scattered on the ground, but these too were untouched.

'I'm very keen to find out who the other girl in the photograph is,' said Fitz, accepting the glass of gin and tonic. 'Garden or sitting room?'

'I'd prefer the kitchen. The Aga keeps it cosy in here,' said Alina, sipping from her own drink. 'It wasn't as warm as the forecast promised, was it?'

'I didn't go for a wander around the garden with our hostess and no jacket,' Fitz remarked. 'And then, to cap it all, you just went for a poke around her bedroom.'

'I did not go in her bedroom,' Alina retorted. 'The photographs were hung on the landing wall for anyone to see. Perhaps I should have used the downstairs facilities, but...' she shrugged and tilted her head to the left, giving Fitz a smile.

'You're sure they were sisters? Not cousins, perhaps?'

'I know cousins can look alike, but I'm convinced they were sisters. Something in the way they were sitting,' she said, thinking about how she and her younger sister Sophie were forced to smile for family photographs.

'Were? You suspect that something has happened to the other girl in the photograph.'

'I do. I wanted to take a snap of it, but I left my phone downstairs.'

'Your phone?' Fitz furrowed his brow.

'Yes, my mobile has a camera application. Doesn't yours?'

'It might. I'll get my nephew to show me. He's rather good at that stuff.'

Alina nodded thoughtfully, watching the blackbird peck at the cake crumbs and spit them out.

'Something on your mind?'

'Hmm, no. Just watching the birds. They're very fussy today. I left some cake out and they won't eat it.'

'It's probably poisoned,' Fitz chortled.

'That's not even remotely funny,' Alina replied. She took another sip of her gin. 'What are we doing here, Fitz? Shouldn't we leave this to the police? I'm sure they're quite capable.'

'I'm sure of that too, Alina, but are the people of this town going to tell the police the sorts of things they reveal to you? I think not.'

'Fine,' said Alina. 'But instead of digging into Fiona's past we're probably better off focusing on who killed Kitty.'

'If you say so,' replied Fitz. He rose, shoving his hands

deep into his pockets. 'But there's something about the Pomeroys I don't like. Ralph was very cagey about his relationship with Kitty. Perhaps he'd respond better to a woman's touch. You need to get him on his own.'

Alina saw Fitz to the front door and waved goodbye. Wandering into the kitchen, she finished her gin and picked up her dustpan and brush. *If the birds aren't going to eat the cake, I'll have to clear it away. Otherwise, there'll be rats.*

She opened the patio door, approached the bird table, and swept the cake into the pan. As she knelt to collect cake crumbs from the path, she saw the tiny sparrow. Lying on its back on the flower bed, with its miniscule talons clenched, it was clearly dead. Tears pricked her eyes. *Have I caused this death?* She cast around for more crumbs, ensuring she gathered them all and threw them into the dustbin. Then she pushed aside the soft earth and covered the sparrow, muttering a short prayer over the body. All the time she cleared away the cake, Alina pushed thoughts from her mind, anxious to avoid the reality that Fitz had been correct. The cake was poisoned, and it had been meant for her.

Despite her fears over the cake situation, as agreed with Fitz, the following morning Alina drove to the golf club to speak with Ralph Pomeroy. She still hadn't decided what pretext she was going to use to get him to give her some time, and wasn't even sure if he would talk about his wife, but she knew she was getting closer to the truth.

When she arrived, Ralph was still out on the course. She decided to wait, and strolled into the dancehall that had been used for the dinner-dance. Was it only two weeks ago? It seemed like so much longer. She stood in the spot where the table had been. Although not superstitious it felt disrespectful to stand on the spot where Kitty had died. There were no flowers to mark the spot and no flowers outside the golf club either. Were the people of Eastwold too prudish to adopt this seemingly new fashion or, as Alina suspected, was it more evidence of how much Kitty Blenkinsop was universally despised?

As far as Alina knew, no one had come forward as next of kin to claim her body or her fortune. Simon Sillitoe, the local solicitor, was keeping quiet on the subject naturally, but all efforts were being made to find someone. Alina wondered if Kitty had any relatives.

She was on the point of calling Fitz to say that the idea of visiting Ralph was a waste of time when the man himself walked into the room.

'I'm told you wanted to see me, Vicar,' Ralph called.

From the far end of the room she waved and trotted the length of the dancehall to join him. 'Oh, yes,' she said. 'I wanted your view on the next fundraiser.'

Ralph held the door open for her, raising his eyebrows. 'Is that the best excuse you could come up with?'

Alina blushed.

'Come to my office,' Ralph said. 'Then you can come straight to the point.'

Head bowed, Alina followed him to his office.

'Drink?' His tone was brusque and didn't invite a long conversation.

'It's a bit early for me, Ralph,' Alina replied. 'But I've not been out on the golf course, like you,' she added, reminding herself she'd get nothing out of him if she antagonised him.

He nodded and poured himself a large whisky from a bottle on top of his filing cabinet.

'Now, come on. What do you really want to talk about?' He fell into his chair and, not for the first time, Alina wondered how many drinks he'd already had.

'Kitty Blenkinsop.' Alina decided that it was best to come

straight to the point, since her attempt at subterfuge had failed.

'What about her?' growled Ralph.

'Were you close?'

Ralph raised his glass and swallowed half the glass of whisky in one gulp. 'I think you know the answer to that, Vicar.'

'And Tracy Goring?'

'Ah, you've been listening to the old biddies down at the Women's Guild, have you?' He swallowed the rest of the whisky and got up from behind his desk. He poured what remained in the bottle into his glass and, after holding it up to the light, he slammed the glass down and pulled open a drawer in the cabinet and retrieved another bottle of whisky. He twisted the top to crack the seal, raised his eyebrows, giving the bottle a puzzled look and then filled his glass up. He sat back down, placed the glass on the blotter in front of him and twisted the glass around. 'I'm not the child's father,' he said finally.

'I see,' said Alina. 'Do you know who is?'

Ralph shook his head and gulped down more whisky.

He coughed, and Alina waited as he cleared his throat. 'I have a couple of suspects in mind. The groundskeeper's nephew and a sous chef we had at the time. Both young. Both good looking.' Ralph opened the top button of his shirt and eased his tweed tie. He ran his fingers around the inside of the short collar. Sweat beaded on his upper lip. His face flushed.

Heart attack? Alina thought, rising from her chair, but Ralph wasn't clutching his left arm in the manner of the classic symptoms. His cherry-red face was symptomatic of something Alina had seen all too recently.

She reached towards him, but before she could make Ralph vomit, he retched on his own, covering the blotter pad and most of the desk. Then, with a thump, he slumped to the floor.

Alina smelt whisky and the unmistakable hint of almonds coming from the blotter.

Kneeling beside him, Alina felt for Ralph's carotid pulse, even though she knew it was pointless. She yanked open his office door and screamed for help.

CHAPTER TWENTY-FIVE

After telling Dot Seward everything, Alina pulled her mobile phone from her bag, called the emergency services, and then placed a call to Richard Laidlaw. She was unsure whether to wait with the body or to sit outside in the corridor.

There was a soft knock on the door. Dot Seward. 'I've made you a cup of tea, Vicar,' she said. 'Do you want to drink it here or in the kitchen?'

Alina hesitated. 'I think I'll sit in here,' she replied. She rose and took the tea from Dot. The cup rattled in its saucer and Alina used both hands to prevent the china crashing to the floor. 'There's nothing to fear from the dead.'

Dot grimaced at the teacup and arched her eyebrows. 'If you say so, Vicar,' she replied. 'I'd as soon wait somewhere else.' She closed the door softly.

Is she trying to avoid awakening the dead? Alina gazed at Ralph with his cherry-red face. A trace of vomit marked his chin. Alina wanted to wipe it away, to give the man some dignity in death, but she knew she shouldn't touch him. Ralph was always such a well-turned-out man. His white handkerchief poked out of his breast pocket, the obligatory half inch of fabric stark even against the tweed of his jacket. She turned her gaze to his lapel and pursed her lips. Where was the fresh buttonhole flower? Ralph always had a single bud pinned to his lapel. Had it fallen out when he fell to the floor? Alina rose and looked around the office. No flower to be seen, but it was odd. Perhaps he'd forgotten today? Alina tapped her fingertips on the desk. No! She remembered the conversation. He always wore a flower to remind him of his Fifi. So why wasn't he wearing one today? It was wrong; it didn't fit. She reached over Ralph's desk, picked up the letter opener and lifted the lapel up, pushing it over with the tip of the letter opener. The pin which held the bud in place was still there. A long pin with a large coloured head.

Exactly the type of pin Amy Pretty favoured for her quilting projects.

Alina knelt on the floor beside Ralph's body. She wanted to snatch the pin up. It was exactly the evidence Richard would use to convict Amy. She reached out towards the pin and then pulled her hand back. She stared at it. It was damning evidence. Utterly damning. *What should I do?* She opened up the camera app on her phone and took a photograph of the pin, but on hearing Richard's voice in the corridor, she grabbed the pin and stuffed it in her pocket.

Calmly, she began to open the door when Richard burst into the room.

'You,' he said. 'Another murder and you're here again. You're not making life easy for yourself, are you, Vicar?'

'I can assure you that I had nothing to do with this man's death,' Alina replied with all the courage she could muster. It wasn't much, but she was not going to let him browbeat her.

'No?' said Richard. 'I'll be the judge of that. After all, it's not the first time you've played a part in a man's death, is it?'

Alina paled. *He must have found out. Of course he'd found*

out. He's a police officer. How much effort or time would it take him to discover I was arrested when Jake had disappeared?

'You've been checking up on me, Inspector,' said Alina. She let out a deep breath. 'I was never charged with anything in relation to my husband's disappearance.'

'I know,' Richard replied. 'But I still had to dig into your past. You understand that, don't you?'

Was he asking *her* forgiveness? 'I had nothing to do with Ralph's murder,' Alina said quietly.

'How do you know it was murder?' DI Laidlaw placed his hands on his hips, glaring at her.

'He was drunk; I saw that as soon as I sat down. He finished one bottle of whisky, then he got another from his drawer, had one swig and dropped down dead. If that's not murder, then I don't know what is. Unless you think he was trying to kill himself?' Alina found her hands hovering close to her hips, mirroring Laidlaw's pose. She clasped her hands together in front of her — a more reverential pose, she decided. How very different this was from their earlier conversation.

'He drank from the second bottle, and dropped down dead?' DI Laidlaw said.

'Yes, Inspector.'

'Was it a new bottle?'

'I supposed so. He took it out of the cabinet and it appeared to be full.' Alina closed her eyes, reliving the scene. Ralph lifting one bottle, finding it empty, getting the new bottle, opening it. That was it! 'The bottle must have been open already. I didn't hear the seal crack but I do recall that he gave it an odd look.'

'So it had been tampered with?'

'That would be my guess, Inspector, but it's not exactly evidence, is it? He might have opened the bottle before and forgotten about it.' Alina shrugged. 'Tell me, do I need to be standing for this interrogation?'

Richard waved her to a seat and she dropped into it, starting when the pin in her pocket dug into her thigh. It was already pricking at her conscience, and now it had stabbed her leg. Should she tell him? But she decided against it. Although there was evidence against Amy Pretty, Alina's instinct told her the old lady was not a killer. *It's as if someone's setting her up for these murders. But who would do that?*

'It looks like the same cause of death as Kitty,' Alina remarked, mildly.

'I can't jump to conclusions.' Richard plunged his hands into his trouser pockets and paced. 'You're right, of course; the two deaths do look similar. Which is a shame, as I had Pomeroy in my crosshairs for Kitty's death.'

'Why? She only humiliated him over seating arrangements,' Alina retorted. 'That's not worth killing over.'

'No, it isn't. I'd wondered if refusing to sleep with him pushed him over the edge? I'll suppose we'll never know now.' Richard continued to pace, idly kicking the worn carpet. 'I know most of the village hated her, but again, that's all very petty and doesn't seem to be a good enough motive for murder.'

She was a blackmailer, Alina wanted to say; however, that only pointed the guilt back at Amy. Or Tracy Goring—someone else Alina couldn't visualise as a murderer. 'Well, if that's all, Inspector,' said Alina. 'I have a lot to do today.'

'Yes, you can go. After all, I know where to find you.'

Alina frowned and turned on her heel. If that was an attempt at levity, it was a remarkably poor one.

CHAPTER TWENTY-SIX

Alina drove to the church. Still shaky after seeing Ralph fall to the floor, she needed the calm that St Edmund's gave her. She knelt at the altar, breathing in the smokiness of long extinguished candles mixed with the scent of old books.

When she'd finished praying, she pushed herself to her feet and turning, she spotted Major Fitzgerald seated in the final row of pews. 'Fitz, did you want something?' she said.

'As a matter of fact, I did.' He stood and ambled towards her. His face was saddened. Had he heard already?

'Have you heard about Ralph Pomeroy?'

'No, what should I have heard?' Fitz furrowed his bushy eyebrows into a fuzzy grey caterpillar.

'He's been poisoned too,' said Alina. 'Looks the same as Kitty's murder.' She held on to the edge of the pew.

Fitz rose and cupped her elbow in his hand. 'Let's get you a cup of tea,' he said. 'Good for shock apparently, though you're a nurse, so you'd know that.'

'Vestry,' Alina whispered. 'Not too much sugar.'

He held onto her arm and supported her to the vestry

office. Clattering cups and saucers, he finally poured a strong cup of tea and had even found the biscuit tin, hidden in Joanne's hidey-hole behind the catering sized tea bags.

Alina sipped her tea. There was no sugar, and although she could feel her body coming down from the adrenaline rush, she didn't need it. Biscuits, they always worked much better in Alina's opinion.

'Why were you here?'

'I did that digging into Fiona's past as we discussed,' he said. 'Very interesting.'

'Relevant?' Alina said. She finished her tea and poured herself another from the pot.

'In the light of what's just happened, very, I'd say.' Fitz brushed his fingers across his moustache before taking a gulp of tea. He reached inside his breast pocket and pulled out a leather-bound notebook.

'As you thought,' he began. 'The girls in the photographs were sisters. But the younger one, Penny, drowned when they were children.'

'How sad,' said Alina. She thought of her own boisterous and somewhat scatty sister with affection. They'd been so close as children. She should ring her this evening for a quick catch up.

'There was something of an age gap between the girls, around eight or nine years from what I understand. Fiona felt left out.'

'Where do you get all this information, Fitz?' said Alina. 'This sounds like something that should be confidential. Hospital records or suchlike.'

'I can't reveal my sources. But I did find out a great deal from the inquest transcript.' Fitz coloured slightly and tapped the side of his nose. 'Do you want to hear the rest of it or not?'

Alina nodded. 'Go on,' she said.

'I understand that Fiona was invited on a picnic with her friends. They invited Penny too but Fifi—that's what the little sister called her—didn't want to take her. The story goes that Fiona argued with her friends and was sitting by the riverbank when Penny, who had followed them, made her appearance. According to witnesses they played together and Penny wanted to swim. Fiona got into the river with her, but only stayed in for a short time. When Penny got into trouble, Fiona leapt in the water to save her little sister but was ultimately unsuccessful.'

'That's awful. She must be carrying all that guilt even though she was only a child herself.'

'Well, Vicar, that's where it gets interesting...'

Alina raised her eyebrows and gave Fitz a wan smile. 'What else did the witnesses have to say?'

'There was, in fact, another witness — a neighbour who knew the family. He was cycling past and saw the girls in the river. He jumped off his bike and ran to help, but by the time he got there it was all over. But this is the interesting bit: at the inquest he said that Fiona wasn't helping her sister, but that she was holding her sister under the water. He said Fiona was trying to kill Penny and that she was successful.'

'Oh my goodness,' said Alina. 'What happened after that? Was Fiona arrested?'

'She was. She was fifteen at the time. She was also charged, but the case didn't go to court. It seems the neighbour withdrew his statement—no idea why—and therefore, she didn't go to prison. However, she was sent to a special school—a psychiatric unit—and she was there until her early twenties. Then she was released. Cured, apparently.'

'Apart from the eyewitness, was there any other evidence?' Alina asked.

'No, nothing more, from what I can gather. But it's clear

we have a potential murderer in our midst. And we went to tea with her!' Fitz guffawed at his own joke.

'I'm not sure it's that funny,' said Alina. She sipped her tea, shuddering as it had gone cold. She stood, pushing the chair back, its legs grating against the stone floor.

A gasp came from outside the half-open vestry office door. Footsteps clattered down the aisle, fading into the distance.

'Oh, a spy,' said Fitz, slapping his hands on his knees. 'What fun. I wonder who was listening to our little chat?'

'It's not funny, Fitz. Who *was* that?' Alina scrabbled towards the door, but the church was empty. Whoever had been listening to them had got away. Only the echo of their footsteps hung in the air. 'How much do you think they heard?'

'Enough, probably. You need to be careful, Alina,' said Fitz.

'I will be,' she replied. 'Listen, I did something that I shouldn't have done. It's been worrying me ever since.' She pulled the pin from her purse and held it up.

'Steady on, Vicar,' he laughed. 'You're not going to stick it in me, are you? I thought that was just for dolls and suchlike.'

'Don't be silly, Fitz,' Alina said. 'I found it on Ralph's body. It's one of Amy Petty's long quilting pins. She uses them to hold all three layers of the project together before the actual quilting is done.'

Fitz blinked. His eyes had glazed over. 'Why do *you* have it?' he asked. 'Why did Ralph have one of Amy's pins? And, much more importantly, why did you take it from a crime scene?'

'I don't know. It all happened in a rush. I noticed Ralph wasn't wearing his usual buttonhole. Then I wondered if it had fallen out, so I checked to see if the pin was there. Remember how he showed us his buttonhole when we went to tea? He just had a plain pin. Not one like this.' Alina pushed the pin in front of his nose. 'I think this was a plant. I think someone is trying to frame Amy. Whoever that was is a cruel and wicked person.'

'Which is all the more reason why you need to be careful, Alina,' said Fitz. 'I'd never forgive myself if anything happened to you.'

Alina patted his hand. 'I can take care of myself,' she said. 'I've been doing it for a long time.'

CHAPTER TWENTY-SEVEN

Alina arrived at the GP surgery for her list of calls for the day and to stock up her medical bag. She frowned at the dark blue car taking up her parking space, but shrugged and found a free bay in the patients' car park. She lugged the heavy bag into the surgery reception area.

Seda beckoned her over. 'That dishy detective is in with Dr McCarthy. He said to send you in when you arrived.'

'Did he now?' replied Alina, pertly. She pursed her lips. *Who does he think he is?* However, she left her medical bag behind the reception desk under Seda's beady eye and strode to Dr McCarthy's consulting room. She knocked, waited a moment, and then walked in.

'Alina, there you are.' Miriam McCarthy beamed at her. 'DI Laidlaw has just been asking about poisons and their effects on people.'

Alina returned Miriam's smile and sat in the other plastic chair facing her. 'Do we know what killed Ralph Pomeroy yet?'

'Toxicology has come back. Cyanide. Same as Kitty. A big dose, too.'

'Have you got anyone in your sights, Inspector?' Alina said, turning to Miriam. 'The inspector used to be quite the marksman when he was in the army.'

'Oh, a military man. How exciting,' cooed Dr McCarthy. 'So do you have any suspects? Surely not Alina still?'

Alina cast an eye in DI Laidlaw's direction. *Was he blushing?*

DI Laidlaw covered his mouth with his hand to cough and clear his throat. 'No, I don't think Nurse Merrycott had the motive to kill any of the victims,' he said. 'She does have an unfortunate habit of being close at hand for the murders though.'

'That's hardly my fault, Inspector,' Alina replied. 'In any case, not only do I not have motive, I don't have the means either.'

'Well, that's not entirely true, is it?' replied the inspector. 'You told *me* that the cyanide was at the golf club. I checked with PC Rigg and, according to him, everyone in the village knows where the cyanide is kept, and that the lock on the door has been broken for months. It's blown the case wide open. The Detective Chief Inspector from HQ in Ipswich is coming to take over the case next week. I'm driving there to meet with her after we've finished here. She wants to know about my progress so far.'

'Have you talked to Fiona Pomeroy yet?' Alina asked.

'Yes, of course. She was the first person I spoke to after I'd talked to everyone at the golf club. Why?'

Alina noticed DI Laidlaw's lips were drawn into a thin line. Did he think she was trying to do his job for him? 'So she's told you about her past? About her sister's death?'

'She has. She was sent to a psychiatric unit for treatment. The case against her was dropped — an unreliable eyewitness, it seems. So they had to let her go.'

'At least she volunteered the information,' Alina said.

'Not quite,' replied Richard. 'I asked her about it. She had no choice. Like I said to you, I've investigated the background of all the people involved in this case. I know a lot about everyone in this town, including you Vicar.' He rose, nodded, and departed.

Alina glowered at the closing door. Insufferable man, she thought, not for the first time.

'What on earth did he mean by that, Alina?' asked Miriam. 'What has he got on you?'

'He's been digging into my past.' Alina reached forward and took a tissue from the box on Miriam's desk. She twisted it in her hands, not quite sure where to begin.

'What is said in this room is said in confidence, Alina. I'd hoped we'd become friends too.' Miriam pulled her chair closer and took Alina's hand, giving it a gentle squeeze.

'I haven't been totally honest with you,' Alina began. 'I am a widow, but only legally. Jacob, my husband—although he preferred to be called Jake—disappeared, twelve years ago. He's never been found and nor has his body. I had him declared dead, just before I came here.'

'Why wait so long?' Miriam murmured.

'That's what my father kept asking. He wanted me to get on with my life, and, to an extent, I have. After Jake left, I focused on Claire and on my career. I found solace with God, eventually applying to join the ministry. But—'

'But a part of you kept clinging to the past?'

Alina nodded. 'Even now, Claire doesn't think he's dead. She said so last time she was home for the weekend.'

'How do you feel about that?'

'Terrified. Jake was involved with some... shall we say... interesting characters.'

'Criminals?'

'Yes, I think so. He didn't work a proper job, but he always had money. I suppose it was the wild side of him I liked. I had done ever since...' Alina paused, blinking her tears away.

'Since?' Miriam prompted. She went to the consulting room sink, ran the tap, and filled a plastic cup with water.

Alina took it and drank thirstily. 'I ran away from home when I was sixteen. Exams were coming up and I felt under a lot of pressure. My parents had high expectations of me. I arrived in London fresh from the provinces and that's when I first met Jake. He found me at Paddington Station and took me to a squat he was living in.'

Miriam tensed, and it was Alina's turn to squeeze the doctor's hand. 'It was nothing like that. He did take care of me. After a few days, I went back to Bournemouth and did my exams, did my A levels, and went to uni. Jake kept in touch. He gave me an address that I could write to, and when I took up my first nursing appointment in London, we got together.'

'Happily ever after?' Miriam gave her a gentle smile.

'No, not quite, but we did get married when I was pregnant with Claire. We'd been living in London but I wanted to be close to family. Jake hated that, and he changed. I suppose he felt trapped by marriage, a baby, and even by my family. Then one day he walked out the door and... I suppose he kept walking. Except—'

'Except?'

'He was never found. Not alive or dead. He didn't take any money from our joint bank account. My father soon made me change everything to my own account, so that if Jake ever returned he'd not be able to clean me out. My parents never liked him but at least they love Claire.' Alina paused, drank the rest of the water, and blew her nose. 'So, now you know everything.'

'And now so does the dishy inspector,' said Miriam. 'But I think you can trust both of us to keep your secret.'

Alina pulled a clean tissue from the box and covered her face, ashamed of keeping part of her secret past hidden from Miriam. She'd done the same to her family. They were convinced that Jake's criminal associates had killed him. Alina knew they hadn't, because, for several weeks after his disappearance, they returned regularly to her house to look for him.

Smiling weakly at Miriam McCarthy, Alina trembled, terrified about how much of her past would be dug up by Detective Inspector Laidlaw.

CHAPTER TWENTY-EIGHT

Alina heaved her medical bag onto Delia's back seat. She drove away from the small town towards Cedric Mahoney's cottage. Her mind was buzzing with the conversations of the last few days. Who would want both Kitty and Ralph dead? It made no sense. There was nothing between them—or was there? Ralph had some reason to hurt Kitty. She'd refused his advances, spread gossip about him and humiliated him. Was that enough to kill her? And Ralph? He was a snob and a bore. He thought he was a ladies' man but was little more than a joke. It might irritate a wife, but enough to commit murder over?

All too soon, Alina arrived at Cedric's cottage. She knocked on the door, watching another flake of paint float to the ground. There was no answer. He must be alone. She retrieved the front door key from the Key Master screwed to the doorpost, unlocked the door, and replaced the key.

'Cedric?' she called. 'Mr Mahoney?' No answer. She walked down the tiny hallway to the sitting room, the room where he spent most of his time.

He was fast asleep in his chair. The walking stick, or club, as Alina thought of it, had fallen to the floor.

Alina picked it up and moved it out of his reach. She placed her hand on his forearm and shook it gently.

Cedric's eyes flew open. 'What are you doing here? How'd you get in?' He reached for his walking stick, his arms flailing. Alina was reminded of an upturned insect, and she bit the inside of her lip. Laughing was not going to help this situation.

'I'm here to check your feet, Mr Mahoney. To make sure the surgery wounds are healing. I've been here before. Do you remember me?'

The old man narrowed his eyes, squinting at her. 'I'm old, not stupid. Best you get on with it. My programme's on in a bit. I don't want to miss it.'

'It's a good job I came along and woke you then,' said Alina. 'Otherwise you would have slept through it.'

Cedric glared at her.

She took this as a sign of assent, and once again placed a couple of her protective gloves on the floor to stop the stickiness of the carpet getting on her uniform trousers. She placed another pair on her hands and removed the old man's slippers and socks. She shuddered at the smell emanating from the slippers, wondering when he'd last had a new pair. At least the scars on his toe were healing, fading into a faint line of pale pink. The wounds were fully recovered. This could be her last visit, although she would call Kriya again about the state of the place. Mr Mahoney, to put it plainly, stunk like a polecat. She rose and peeled the gloves off her hands and off the carpet.

'I'm going to sign you off, Mr Mahoney,' she said. 'I'll let Dr McCarthy know how well you've healed, but you must keep taking the medication or the gout will come back.'

'What happened with Pomeroy? Did you kill him?'

'I did not.' Alina threw Mr Mahoney's notes into her medical bag, her fists clenched.

'Do you know who did kill him?' Cedric waved his hand towards the old sofa and Alina sat.

'I don't, no,' she sighed.

'Not much of an investigator are you? At least there's not been any other bodies.'

Alina's jaw dropped. 'No, not any people at least.'

Cedric looked up, his head tilted to one side. 'Speak,' he said.

'I found a dead bird in the garden. A sparrow.'

'What killed it? Your cat?'

'I don't think so. Thalia's too lazy to chase birds any longer—' Alina paused, thinking about clearing the cake away and Fitz's comment. Had the cake been poisoned? 'I have to go,' she said.

The old man glowered at her from underneath bushy white eyebrows and nodded at his stick.

Alina rose, packed her bag, ensuring she'd left nothing behind and placed it in the hallway. Then, and only then, did she put the walking stick back in reach of the curmudgeonly old man.

He reached down in the recess of his chair and pulled out the remote control, switched on the television and dismissed her with a wave of his hand.

Alina made her escape. She pulled the front door closed and tested it, then walked to her car. She sat in the driver's seat to call Kriya. No answer, so she left a message and wrote a text.

Have you found him a cleaner or home help yet? He doesn't appear to have washed in days.

About to replace the phone in her pocket, Alina frowned

as it buzzed. She'd saved the contact in her phone. Richard Laidlaw. What on earth did he want?

'Alina,' he said, 'Glad I caught you. I'm going to question Fiona Pomeroy. She's asked for you to sit in on the interview. It's highly irregular, as I'm sure you know, but I think I'm going to allow it. Just this once.'

'Richard, I have calls to make. Patients to see. I can't just drop everything.'

'Oh don't worry, I called the surgery and explained everything to Dr McCarthy. It's fine. They're rearranging your appointments for you. I'll see you at the station in what? Forty-five minutes?'

'Fine,' she hissed. *How dare he? Why does he think it's okay to reorganise my day like this?* She took a deep breath, clasped her hands together on the steering wheel and asked for patience. She let out the breath slowly, allowing the action to remove all stress from her body. She fixed a beatific smile on her face and headed to the police station.

'Thank you for coming, Vicar.' Fiona's eyes were red rimmed and her face blotchy. A far cry from her usual, elegant self.

'I'm not a solicitor, Fiona,' Alina said. 'Are you sure that you'd not be better off with legal advice? I can't give you that. Medical and spiritual, those are my limits.' She folded Fiona's hands in her own, sympathising at the loss of her husband. She knew what that felt like only too well.

'I needed a friend,' Fiona replied, giving Alina a weak smile. 'I know I'm innocent. I just want to know what he's got on me.'

'Possibly nothing. But it's part of their procedure to question everyone close to the… the victim.'

Fiona nodded. She clutched Alina's hand and the two

women waited for DI Laidlaw to speak with them. They didn't have to wait long.

Accompanied by a uniformed female officer, Richard sat opposite them and placed a manila file on the desk. The PC checked the recording device and nodded at him.

After the preliminaries of a police interview, Richard said, 'Why did you kill your husband, Mrs Pomeroy?'

Fiona clenched her fists, her knuckles whiter than her pale face as she covered her mouth. Tears sprung from her eyes and trickled down her cheeks. She accepted the clean tissue that Alina passed to her. 'I didn't kill him,' she said, her words muffled by her tears and sobs. 'I loved my husband. Can't you see how devastated I am?' She faced DI Laidlaw and blinked away the tears in her eyes, causing them to race down her cheeks. They pooled on her chin and dropped onto her fawn skirt, darkening the fabric.

Alina frowned at Richard, but he gave her a very slight shake of his head. *What is he up to?*

'Then how do you account for your fingerprints being on the whisky bottle? The bottle which contained the poison that killed him?'

'I buy the whisky and bring it to the clubhouse for him. It would be odd if my fingerprints weren't on the bottle, Inspector.' Fiona raised her chin, looking as if she'd recovered her senses.

'Is there a reason he doesn't get his whisky from the bar? There is a bar at the clubhouse, isn't there?' DI Laidlaw posed his questions calmly and deliberately. Alina decided Richard wasn't the sort of man to pose any questions he didn't already know the answer to.

'He prefers the whisky that I get him from the wine merchants,' Fiona sniffed.

'Yes, it's quite expensive, isn't it?'

Fiona dipped her head in assent.

'So you'd expect the bottles to be sealed when new, wouldn't you?' Richard lined his pen up with the side of the folder, before staring at Fiona intently.

Fiona puckered her brown. 'I don't understand what you're saying, Inspector,' she said. 'Are you telling me the bottle was tampered with? How?'

'I didn't say the bottle was tampered with, Mrs Pomeroy.' Richard's face was impassive, but he oozed smugness. 'As for how, well, that's how the killer got the poison in the bottle. We've had it tested and the results show it's the same poison used on Mrs Blenkinsop.'

'Are you accusing me of that as well, Inspector?' Fiona's face had regained colour. She was puce with indignation.

'I'm not making any accusations, Mrs Pomeroy. I am merely seeking the truth. I have a witness who says when your husband opened the new bottle the seal didn't break. The witness didn't hear the crack. Therefore, I surmise that the bottle was already open. A bottle containing the poison which killed your husband and which only had yours and his fingerprints on it.'

Fiona turned to stare at Alina. 'I thought you were with Ralph when he died? Are you this witness? I thought I could trust you!' Fiona stood, her chair clattering to the floor. 'I think I'd rather continue this conversation with my solicitor after all, if you don't mind, Inspector.'

'I understand.' Richard smiled politely. 'If you'll just wait here. Stop the tape please, PC Robbins, and stay here with Mrs Pomeroy until her solicitor arrives, will you?'

'Of course, Sir. Interview terminated at fifteen thirty-five,' she said, before clicking the recording device off.

CHAPTER TWENTY-NINE

Alina followed Richard into the corridor.

'Why did you make me do that?' she said. 'What were you *thinking*?'

Richard leaned against the beige wall, placing the sole of his shoe against the wall. He rubbed his hands over his face. His skin was grey, dark shadows stark under his red-rimmed eyes.

Alina looked away and, wanting to stay angry with him, she focused her attention on her surroundings. She glanced up the corridor, at the scuff marks on the lower section. The skirting boards were grey with mop marks. 'Well?' she said. 'What are you playing at?'

'I was hoping I'd get somewhere with you there. I suppose I hoped she'd give me a good lead. Now I'm going to have to hand this case over to DCI Ratcliffe.' He dropped his foot to the floor, leaning over to rest his hands on his knees.

'Why is that a problem? You've known for a few days you needed to hand the case over. What's with you and DCI Ratcliffe?'

Richard stood up, sighed, and placed his hands on Alina's shoulders. 'She's my ex-wife,' he said.

Alina glanced at his hands on her shoulders and, puzzled, she stared at him again. 'I see.'

'She called last night. She can't wait to take on this case and show me up.' Richard folded his arms. 'I can't let her do that.'

Driving into the centre of Eastwold, Alina was unsure how she felt about the prospect of Richard's ex-wife, and decided she needed cheering up. She parked Delia in the market square, trying to determine what would cheer her most. She peeked around the door of the café, but it was full. Not a spare table anywhere. However, at the far end of the High Street a new café had opened, and she'd not been in there so far. *Time to give it a try.*

As she drew closer to the freshly painted door, she passed Pretty's Yarns and Fabrics. The shop remained closed while Amy was recuperating. Alina hoped the old lady would be better soon.

She pushed open the café door, assailed by the scent of fresh coffee and cakes. Wonderful, she thought. This café was also very busy, but she spied an empty table near the back. Settling herself into the chair, she picked up the menu.

'What'll it be?' Hair scraped off her face, dressed in black with a black pinafore, Tracy Goring stood before her with a notepad and pencil.

'Tracy! What are you doing here?' Alina asked.

'I needed a job. Flowers by Fifi is closed while Fiona is in mourning. She's asked me to help with the flowers for the funeral, but I can see her heart isn't in the business anymore.' Tracy shuffled her feet.

'And the children?'

'Ethan's home. Mum's also out of hospital now. She's feeling better, so she'll pick the older ones up and I'll be home not long after. That way she's not alone with them too long.'

'I'm so pleased.' Alina smiled at Tracy's pale face. 'Scrambled egg on granary toast and coffee, thanks.' She replaced the menu on the table and gazed at her surroundings. An old-fashioned shelf had been installed around the room. It sat close to the ceiling and held various handmade items from the pottery, small oils from a local artist, and stuffed toys. Judging by the small white tags attached to each, they were for slae.

Just as Tracy returned with her coffee, Fitz took the chair on the other side of the table.

'I thought that was you,' he said. 'I have news.'

'I'm beginning to think you're stalking me, Fitz. Anyway, is it safe to talk in public?' Alina leaned towards him, her voice *sotto voce*.

'Probably safer here than your vestry. At least we can see if anyone is listening in,' Fitz said.

Tracy returned with a plate of fluffy scrambled eggs on toast and the major decided to have the same.

'What news do you have?' asked Alina, sliding the napkin onto her lap.

'The blackmail is a non-starter,' Fitz whispered. 'No large sums either in or out of Kitty's bank account.'

'Does anyone benefit financially from her death?' Alina scooped a morsel of egg onto her fork and popped it into her mouth while she waited for an answer.

Fitz shrugged. 'She'd not made a will. She didn't need to as Reg's will transferred everything to his nephew in the event of Kitty's death.'

'She had no family at all? That's sad,' said Alina.

'My snooping uncovered some family, but Kitty had

fallen out with them all years ago.' Fitz leaned away from the table as Tracy laid his toast and eggs in front of him. 'They're not interested,' he said, picking up knife and fork, ready to tuck in.

'So sad,' said Alina.

Conversation gave way to eating and Alina sipped her second cup of coffee as she watched him tuck in. If no one was going to come forward to make decisions about Kitty's funeral, then it fell to the local authority to arrange a simple service. Alina decided to approach the council and offer to officiate. At least Kitty's estate would be able to cover the costs.

Fitz placed his knife and fork down on the plate with a clatter.

'If blackmailing isn't the reason Kitty was killed, then what was?' Alina said. 'Jealousy?'

'Or revenge,' said Fitz. 'Amy still fits the profile.'

'Linda fits the jealousy profile,' Alina replied. 'Yet who would want Ralph dead? I mean, we are assuming both deaths are linked?'

'The same method was used,' said Fitz. 'I agree there has to be a link, but like you, I can't see what it is.'

CHAPTER THIRTY

Alina crossed the green, waving a greeting to Fiona Pomeroy who was dead-heading roses in her front garden. Fiona waved back, although, Alina noticed, she did so with secateurs still grasped in her right hand.

Wandering up and down the pews, Alina collected prayer books and straightened the kneelers. When she had an armful of books, she strolled to the back of the pews and placed the prayer and hymn books in their correct places on the bookshelf. She walked up the nave, her footfalls echoing throughout the building, and sat in the front pew, scratching her head.

I know the answer, she muttered to herself, thinking about the footsteps she'd heard running away a few days ago. There was something familiar about the echo made by the listener's shoes. She raised her hand and rubbed the back of her neck. It helped ease some of the tension, but she was getting a headache from running all the various scenarios through her head. It seemed everyone in the entire town knew about the broken lock and the cyanide. She jumped as a wasp landed on her sleeve. Standing slowly, she shook her sleeve, hoping to remove the creature without any harm to either of them. It dropped to the floor, unmoving. Alina nudged it with her toe, but the wasp was dead.

'Oh, good grief,' she said. 'That's it. That's who killed him.' She pulled her cassock up to her waist so she could grab her mobile phone.

'I wouldn't do that if I were you, Alina.'

Alina gazed heavenwards and closed her eyes. Blast, she thought. Aloud, she said, 'Hello Fiona. What a lovely surprise.'

'Is it, Alina?'

Alina faced her companion but was disconcerted to see that the large pair of secateurs remained in Fiona Pomeroy's hand.

Fiona flicked the secateurs irritably and Alina stepped into the aisle. 'Where are we going, Fi?' she said.

'Just walk, Vicar,' Fiona said. 'I hate being called Fi. That's what my sister called me.'

Alina headed down the aisle at a measured pace, feeling the point of the secateurs near her kidneys. As they neared the porch, Alina slowed, but Fiona dug the secateurs sharply into her back. 'Tower,' she said.

Alina swallowed but didn't argue. She tried to make herself stroll calmly towards the heavy wooden door, behind which were the stairs for the church tower. Shaking, she scarcely noticed the coldness of the heavy, Middle Ages iron clasp. She placed her hand on the rope banister rail and, gripping it tightly, began to trudge up the stone staircase. Alina panted, hauling herself up each step as she clung to the rope rail. Her thigh muscles and her lungs were burning as they reached the level of the bells. She kept staring ahead, not daring to look at the bells in case she caught a glimpse of the void beneath them. She rested for a moment, but the point of the secateurs jabbed sharply against her spine. Alina squealed.

'Keep going, Vicar. We're nearly there,' muttered Fiona.

'What are you going to do?'

Fiona didn't speak, but her ragged breath was hot on Alina's neck.

With gritted teeth, Alina grasped the rope again and continued her ascent. She tried to control her breathing, but her heart was pounding both from fear and exertion. If I get out of this, I promise I'll lose weight, she thought to herself. Head down, she carried on plodding up the stone steps. There were no windows on the stairway but there was a pinprick of light from the feeble overhead bulbs. She stopped to catch her breath, but the prodding secateurs became insistent, and reluctantly she pressed on.

The stairway came to an end. The doorway ahead was a new fire door with a security bar. Alina hung onto the bar to keep herself upright but, as Fiona pushed her, the door swung open and ahead she saw the castellated balustrade surrounding the peaked, lead roof of the church tower. Above their heads, the giant cross moved gently in the wind. From its base, a green strip of lightning rod ran down the roof over the balustrade and continued down the outside of the tower.

Alina sunk to her knees, grasping for breath.

'Ever nearer to your God, hey Vicar. Isn't this great?' shouted Fiona.

Still on her knees, unable to catch her breath, Alina nodded. Despite the bright sunshine, the wind was chilly. Even protected by the balustrade, the breeze caught her hair and tried to tease it out of the bun at the nape of her neck.

'Get up!' shouted Fiona.

'I can't!' Alina gasped.

'Get up!' Fiona said again, leaning over her victim and pressing the points of the secateurs against Alina's throat.

Alina gulped as the sharp points cut her skin. She placed her left hand on the stonewall surrounding them and, using her right hand, she pushed herself to her feet. She took one look at the view and, vision blurring, sank to the ground.

'Still afraid of heights, Alina?' Fiona grinned and peered over the edge. She waved, but from her prone position Alina had no idea if anyone waved back.

Alina turned around into a sitting position, her feet braced against the balustrade and her back against the lead roof. 'Why did you do it?' she said.

'Do what?'

'Kill Kitty.'

Fiona shrugged. 'Ralph.'

'But she had affairs with lots of men. It meant nothing to her. Ralph was just one in a long line. Couldn't you find it in yourself to forgive him?'

'You don't understand, Vicar. I wasn't jealous of an affair. She rejected Ralph. Humiliated him at every opportunity. She was a hideous woman. I wanted to make her suffer,' replied Fiona. 'I hadn't poisoned anyone before. I didn't know how much to use. I wanted to give her a long, lingering, painful death. I hear ricin is good for that, but it's rather difficult to get hold of.'

'Yes,' Alina muttered. 'There's a very good reason for that.'

'Then Ralph complained about the lock being broken at the golf club.' Fiona remained at the balustrade staring into the distance. 'I knew from having the wasps nest dealt with about the cyanide that was kept in there. It seemed like providence was calling me.'

'But why kill her if she wasn't having an affair with him?'

'Because he was mooning around like a lovesick puppy. Pathetic. He couldn't get over it. Unrequited love, I suppose. I suppose I thought that once she was out of the way...' Fiona shrugged.

'But why kill Ralph?'

'Because it made no difference.' Fiona sighed and turned away from the view. She cocked her head and looked at Alina. 'He was still moping over her and what might have been. We argued. That's when he realised I'd killed her. I had to stop him before he went to the police.'

'What are you going to do now?'

'Now?' Fiona shook her head. 'What do you mean?'

'What are you going to do with me?' Alina turned her head to the stairway door. It was half open. Had she really heard footsteps running up the stairs? She clasped her hands together and bowed her forehead to meet them.

'Does praying help?' said Fiona.

'It helps me,' Alina replied.

Fiona glanced at the doorway and Alina wondered if she could hear the footsteps too. She dropped the secateurs to the ground and, as Alina reached out to grab them, the door burst open and Bert Rigg and Fitz stood panting in the doorway.

Bert raised his right hand to Fiona as if asking for a few moments to catch his breath before arresting her. Alina found herself smiling at the bizarre scenario, but Bert's expression changed to one of horror and he leapt forward. Alina turned her gaze to Fiona.

But Fiona was no longer in sight.

CHAPTER THIRTY-ONE

Alina raced to the edge and, without thinking, she looked over the battlements. Fiona's body lay on the ground, twisted like a discarded doll. Alina closed her eyes briefly to whisper a word of forgiveness and ask God to take care of Fiona's soul. Opening her eyes, she stared at the view, looking out over her parish towards the sea. Blue today, like the sky. The vision stretched to the horizon where sky and sea met. She looked landwards at the people below. Little people. Too little. Her knees gave way as the images before her spun, and she sat down heavily. She clasped her hands together on her knees and allowed the tears to flow. She'd been saved, but for what?

Bert and Fitz knelt down beside her.

'How did you know?' she said.

'Mrs Stokes saw you going into the church and Mrs Pomeroy following you. She called me,' said Fitz. 'I called Bert.'

'Are you all right, Vicar?' said PC Rigg.

'Yes, Bert,' she said. 'Yes, I'm fine.'

'Can you stand?'

Nodding, Alina pushed herself to her feet, but leaned against the solid wall behind her. With Fitz's support, she wobbled to the doorway, pausing when she heard the sirens. Although she'd not wish the sight of Fiona's broken body on anyone, she hoped it was Geoff. He'd treat her with respect and dignity even though she was a murderer.

Gripping the heavy rope even more tightly than she had on the walk up the stairs, Alina made her way down, stumbling every so often until Fitz moved ahead of her.

'If you fall, you'll fall into me,' he murmured.

Alina smiled, a short, tight smile. She was exhausted, but knew she had to keep moving. The stress of the situation on the roof had stolen all her energy. Thoughts of slipping under her warm duvet and sleeping for a week seemed like the perfect plan for the very near future.

Keep moving, she told herself. *One step in front of another.* Knuckles white on the rope banister, she kept pushing herself forward until at last she was at the oak door at the bottom of the tower. Fitz pushed the door open and guided Alina to sit down at one of the rear pews.

Jo Stokes bustled forward with a tea tray. She poured a mug, slopped a generous amount of milk in the tea and spooned in three sugars. 'For the shock,' she said.

And to give me late-onset diabetes, thought Alina, but now wasn't the time to worry about diets so she drank it. She was parched. Reaching forward, she poured another mug from the teapot and poured in less milk and one spoonful of sugar. 'Thanks Jo,' she said, about to reach for a biscuit, when running footsteps stopped her.

Richard.

He raced across the narthex and skidded to a halt, kneeling down in front of her. 'Are you okay?' he asked, his eyes wild, hair dishevelled.

'I'm fine,' Alina replied. She patted him on the shoulder

and he placed his hand on top of hers. He raised her hand from his shoulder, his rapid breath warm on the back of her hand. Alina's heart pounded, her mouth dry, and for the briefest of moments she waited for the kiss. She held her breath, tensing her body, and his face darkened.

Then he jumped to his feet. His professional demeanour snapped into place. 'Right, can anyone tell me what happened here?'

'That would be me,' whispered Alina. 'But I might need a moment.'

'You take all the time you need,' Richard replied. 'PC Rigg, I'll hear your report, please. Tell me what you know.'

The two police officers walked away. Alina stared after them.

Fitz coughed politely. 'Shall I take you home, Vicar?'

'Yes please, Fitz. I think I'd like that.'

Fitz held out his hand and pulled her to her feet. She noticed his jaw tense, and hung her head, promising once again that she would lose weight. *On the other hand, you're lucky to be alive.*

'How did you get here today, Vicar?' asked Fitz. 'Cycle, or did you drive that old wreck of yours?'

Alina bristled. More insults for poor Delia. She loved that car and had no plans to replace her. 'I walked,' she heard herself say. Her voice came from a distance. Shock, yet again, she knew. She smiled to herself, thinking that this was supposed to be a quiet little town — a break from bustling London.

Fitz cleared his throat, the noise breaking through her thoughts. 'Shall we?' he said. 'I've got the old jalopy outside.'

She raised her head to smile at him, taking in his bushy eyebrows and the military moustache. He was a good friend, but she had a completely different military man on her mind.

Fitz led her outside to the red sports car. He opened the

door and held it for her as she completed the gymnastic manoeuvre to get into the seat. At least she was wearing trousers today.

They drove back to Lighthouse Cottage in silence. Fitz killed the engine outside and, as the perfect gentleman he was, leapt out to open her door for her. 'I won't come in, Vicar,' he said quietly. 'I think you should get some rest.'

Alina nodded, her mind still buzzing. Rest was the last thing on her mind. She unlocked the door and let herself into the living room. Thalia was stretched out as usual in front of the fireplace, but this time taking advantage of a sunbeam glinting through the window.

Thalia rose, arched her back and padded to the kitchen where she sat expectantly by her full bowl. 'Meow,' she said.

Alina scooped her up and buried her face in the cat's fur.

Thalia placed one paw either side of Alina's neck, resting her head under Alina's chin. She didn't move even when her coat became sodden with tears.

CHAPTER THIRTY-TWO

The sun woke Alina, glinting on her eyelids. She stretched out under the duvet until she met Thalia's solid form. 'What are you doing here?' she asked.

The cat didn't reply but nuzzled her owner's chin, tickling Alina's nose with her fur. She sat back on her haunches and kneaded Alina's chest with her soft brown paws.

Alina lay still, staring into the cat's deep blue eyes. She scratched the cat's tummy through the covers and Thalia frowned. Who says cats don't have expressions? She moved onto her side, pulling her knees up and snuggling the cat against her body.

Thalia arched her back and jumped off the bed. Tail raised, she ambled to the bedroom door and gave Alina a haughty glance before padding regally down the stairs.

'Time to get up, I suppose,' Alina muttered. She swung her feet to the ground, feeling for her slippers, when she noticed that she was still dressed. The curtains were open too, which was unusual. A half-drunk cup of tea was beside the bed. Then it came back to her. All the events of the day before. Her stomach rumbled. She'd not eaten anything when she got home. She'd just made the tea and come to lie on her bed. She'd slept the whole night through and it was now time to face another day and, there was no doubt, a number of questions she would have to answer.

After feeding the cat and herself, Alina showered, dressed in her nurse's uniform, and left for the surgery. She placed her pass card against the ID scanner and the glass doors slid apart. The applause was thunderous. Well, as thunderous as five women can be. Seda, Kriya, Dr McCarthy, Linda Cranford and even Ros Cauthorn clapped.

Alina clasped her hand to her chest, blushing. 'Stop,' she gasped. 'What's all this for?'

'You're still alive and you solved the murders,' Kriya squealed. 'We're so pleased to see you unharmed.'

'I didn't do anything,' said Alina. 'And I was wrong for the most part. I believed it was Amy Pretty for a very long time.' She turned as the glass door slid open behind her. Fitz.

'Come here, Fitz. I couldn't have done any of it without you. How *do* you get all that information on people?' she said to him.

Fitz smirked and tapped the side of his nose again. 'I could tell you, but then I'd have to kill you, and I think there's been enough of that around here, don't you?'

'I couldn't agree more,' said Alina. 'But it nearly went very wrong.'

'What put you onto her?' asked Miriam.

'Wasps,' said Alina. 'A dead wasp in the church. I found it near one of the lovely bouquets that Fiona does... did for the church. Then it all became clear. But, by that point, she had me caught. She told me the rest of it on the tower roof. Before—'

'Don't worry about that, Vicar,' said Fitz, putting his arm around her shoulders. 'We got her in the end.'

Alina gave him a weak smile. Only she knew how close it had come to a very different outcome.

'Oh,' said Seda. 'I nearly forgot. These come for you.' She gave Alina a beautifully wrapped bunch of flowers with a card emblazoned with the Flowers by Fifi logo.

Alina gulped. Was this a sick joke from Fiona? Trembling, she opened the card and read it. Her eyes misted, obscuring the words as tears fell. 'It's little Ethan Goring,' she said. 'He's recovering from the meningitis. The flowers are from Tracy. She used to work for Fiona, you know.'

'That's great news,' said Dr McCarthy. 'Now I suppose we'd all better get to work. Just because we have a sleuth in our midst, patients still need treating.'

Alina smiled, gazing at the flowers. Such a kind thought. She'd go see Tracy later to thank her. She laid the flowers down on the coffee table in the middle of the waiting room, wondering who would do the flowers for Fiona's funeral.

Later, when everyone had left, Alina slipped away. Tracy. Naturally, it would be Tracy who'd prepare the flowers for Fiona's funeral. Driving towards the marsh, Alina did wonder if she'd find the busy young mother at home, but she was lucky.

'I came to say thank you for the flowers,' she began, as Tracy opened the door and beckoned her inside.

'Don't worry. I wanted to say thank you for saving Ethan and I didn't know how else to do it.'

'I am sorry about Fiona.'

Tracy shrugged. 'I'm gonna miss her. She said I reminded her of her little sister.'

'Did she say anything else about Penny?'

'Was that what she was called? No, she never mentioned her again. I think telling me about it in the first place was a mistake. We were doing flowers for a baby's funeral and Fi was really sad that day. Not herself, you know? I don't believe what they're all saying. I don't think she killed her sister.'

'We'll never know,' said Alina. 'That secret died with her. Perhaps it's best if we leave it in the past?'

'Agreed,' replied Tracy.

A few days later, Tracy did attend Fiona's funeral at the crematorium, accompanied by her mother. Apart from Linda Cranford, they were the only mourners. However, that was still two more than had appeared at Kitty Blenkinsop's funeral a few days before. Only Reg Blenkinsop's nephew had showed up. Even that surprised Alina, who had expected to perform the funeral service to an empty room.

Once again, the pallbearers were supplied by the funeral home. They left to smoke outside as soon as they'd laid the coffin on the raised platform.

Alina bowed her head and waited until the last notes of Grieg's *Morning* faded away, then raised her head, gazing at the three women in front of her.

'I am the resurrection and the life,' she began.

CHAPTER THIRTY-THREE

JULY

The church was full. Every single resident from Eastwold who could leave their home was in attendance for Ralph Pomeroy's funeral. It was a glaring contrast to the three mourners at Fiona's funeral.

As she looked out over the crowd, Alina saw Cedric Mahoney in a wheelchair between Tracy Goring and her mother. It was good to see that she'd fully recovered from her stroke. After Fiona's funeral, Tracy had confided that her mother was coming to live with her. Although who was keeping an eye on who wasn't clear. Mrs Blowers had also agreed to take on the cleaning of Cedric's cottage. She was the first person not to run from the house having seen the challenge, and the first person who was able to cope with Cedric's tantrums. Long may it last, thought Alina.

She walked down the aisle to meet the coffin and the pall-bearers: Fitz, Frank Stokes, Simon Sillitoe and Linda Cranford's estranged husband, Nick. When she reached the narthex, she caught Wilf's eye. He immediately sat down, and the first notes of the funeral march filled the church. The procession stepped slowly up the aisle. Was it only a few short weeks ago that she'd performed a wedding here? So much had happened in a short space of time.

The pallbearers laid the coffin on the catafalque near the altar. Alina raised her head and spoke to the congregation.

'I am the resurrection and the life, saith the Lord,' she intoned, exactly as she had at the other recent funerals. 'He that believeth in me, though he were dead, yet shall he live.'

Not a sound could be heard in the pauses. There had been a number of volunteers for the readings, and Alina and Fitz, overwhelmed, had to narrow down a shortlist. Ralph Pomeroy, it appeared, was much more popular in death than in life.

Again, Alina's thoughts drifted to Fiona. A much beloved member of the community in life. Few had come to bid her farewell.

After the committal, Alina stayed at Ralph's graveside until the last clod of earth covered him. Then she turned and followed the path with the rest of the congregation to the gardens of the pub opposite.

On seeing her walk into the garden, Fitz waved and fetched her a gin and tonic from the bar. 'I thought you could do with this, Vicar,' he said. 'It was a good service.'

'Yes,' she said. 'Well attended. Shame the same couldn't be said for poor Fiona. I had hoped—'

'She was a murderer,' said Fitz. 'Even though one of the people she killed wasn't well liked, Fiona was still a murderer.'

'I know,' sighed Alina. 'But she was in a lot of pain. I don't think she could face what she'd done in the end.'

'Or couldn't face the consequences, more like,' snorted Fitz.

'No, I think you're wrong,' Alina said. 'She'd faced the consequences of a murder accusation before, and survived. I don't think she saw a future for herself without Ralph. I believe she cared for him deeply.'

'If you say so, Vicar. If you say so.'

They clinked glasses, and then Alina wandered around the gardens to talk to people. The conversations, however, left her feeling flat and uninspired. She didn't have a second drink but strolled across the road back to the church and sat inside, resting in the choir pews, drinking in the peacefulness of the church. Her stomach rumbled. She needed to eat. She decided to get changed and pick up something on the way home. After hanging her vestments in the vestry, Alina closed the church doors. Jo or Fitz would come along later and lock up for the night. Even in a quiet place like Eastwold, the church was never left unlocked overnight.

Alina returned to Ralph's grave, squinting at the bright sunshine after the cool, low light of the church. The brown mounds of freshly tilled soil rose high over the grass encircling the grave. Alina breathed in the scent of the earth and looked at the empty plot beside Ralph's. Next week she would collect Fiona's ashes from the crematorium and scatter them here. There would be no mention of Fiona on the headstone — she was a murderer, after all. However, the bishop had finally agreed that her ashes could be scattered next to her husband. It was a small victory on the face of it, but a victory, nonetheless.

Alina bent to straighten a bunch of flowers and rose slowly. A wave of loneliness and longing washed over her. Would anyone be there to share her resting place? Once again, her thoughts drifted to Jake, as they had done so many times these past few weeks. *You have to stop living in the past, Alina,* she muttered to herself. *Time to move on.*

She shivered despite the warm sun and, shading her eyes, she looked around the graveyard. All was quiet. Peaceful and serene. Half-turning, Alina caught a glimpse of movement at the kissing gate. She whirled around.

Someone *was* there!

A man, hands deep in his jeans pockets, stared back at her. He raised one hand in greeting.

Alina caught her breath. It had been over twelve years, but the movement seemed familiar. Was it him? Could it be him? But he was dead, wasn't he? He must be dead. Alina grabbed her bag from the ground and ran to the gate. Her smooth soles slipped on the freshly cut grass; she tripped and fell. Pushing herself to her feet, she continued to run. Reaching the gate, she wrenched it open, squeezing herself through the gap where the gate met the half-horseshoe fencing.

Her chest heaved as she gasped for breath. She looked in both directions, but the street was empty. Running to the corner, she looked down Chancery Lane, but there was no one to be seen.

She paced slowly back towards the church, brushing grass cuttings off her jeans. She'd need to scrub them to wash out the grass stains. Heart still pounding, she ran the images of the man through her head. She was certain she'd know that walk anywhere, even though she realised her mind could be playing tricks on her.

As she had often feared, Jake Merrycott was still alive. And he'd found her.

The End

BRITISH ENGLISH

To my lovely readers,

A very long time ago, I was born in Britain. I love this little island and all its quirks. There are some things that I don't love, but they will never be in the Cassie Rush books.

I do use UK English spellings, punctuation, and grammar, including the "u" in colour, humour, rigour and other words I can't think of right now. I also use an "s" where America tends to prefer a "z", such as in cosy/cozy. In fact, my laptop just auto-corrected cozy!

I read a vast number of cosy mysteries written by American writers. I love the sarcasm, humour, and I especially love the paranormal, witchy novels. It's also made me acutely aware of how the grammar differs between the two languages.

I hope you'll forgive me for sticking with the language I've been using all my life.

Thanks,
Cassie

ACKNOWLEDGMENTS

Getting a book ready for publication is a huge team effort, and I'm lucky to be surrounded by such supportive friends and dedicated professionals who make my books the best they can be.

Special thanks go to the following people:

To the Reverend Judy Miller, now retired from nursing but not the clergy, who not only read the book to make sure I'd not made too many errors, but also gave me so many stories and insight into living in a village that there's a wealth of stories still to come.

To Audrey Wiggins (and Hannah, her niece, one of my oldest friends), who helped me understand the workings of the Women's Institute so that I could create the Eastwold Women's Guild. Thank you, Hannah, for the introduction and driving me around that week.

To the fabulous Molly Burton, who created the covers for the Eastwold by the Sea series and for the Kim David series that will be out very soon.

To the Reverend Hannah Barraclough, who via the power of Twitter, introduced me to the phrase "the vicar's knickers". It made me squeal with laughter and I had to include it.

To Julie Nieminen, who's been proofreading my novels for a while now. Apparently they make a nice change from the non-fiction of her day job.

Thanks to my editor who, as usual, made me sit with my head in my hands, wondering if I can actually write.

Finally, a huge thanks to the ARC team, who read through and helped catch the Hide-and-Seek universal champions—the typo. If you find any, let me know. I hate them as much as you do.

Thanks
Cassie
Suffolk, 2022

REVIEWS

I do hope you enjoyed the first excursion to Eastwold by the Sea? If so please could you leave me a review on Amazon or Goodreads? The link for your local Amazon store is below.

Amazon https://mybook.to/wSKod

Thank you
Cassie

ABOUT THE AUTHOR

Hi there, my name is Cassie Rush and I'm a British author of cosy mysteries set in the English country- or seaside.

I absolutely love the coastal town of Southwold which is a short drive up the coast from where I live. It's why I chose to set my popular, *Eastwold by the Sea* series there. Although my version of the town is entirely fictional as I like to move streets around. I hate it when an author sets a story somewhere you know well and gets details wrong, don't you?

I have been a fan of Agatha Christie all my life and I adore the other golden age authors. I especially enjoy the stories of Miss Marple, Father Brown, Brother Cadfael and Lord Peter Wimsey.

I was really lucky at school (let's not talk about how long ago that was though) to have brilliant and enthusiastic history teachers. It's given me a lifelong love of history and all the tales that the past has to offer.

I also write as Caroline Goldsworthy—these books are rather darker with more graphic content.

BVPRI - #0012 - 200423 - C0 - 203/127/11 - PB - 9781916122185 - Matt Lamination